IN AN INSTANT

Kayla Perrin

BET Publications LLC

ARABESQUE BOOKS are published by

BET Publications, LLC
c/o BET BOOKS
One BET Plaza
1900 W Place NE
Washington, D.C. 20018-1211

ISBN 0-7394-2778-4

Printed in the United States of America

For Rose Ficco. I know you wish for more chivalrous times and more chivalrous men. Darren Burkeen's for you.

Prologue

"Oh, Harris." Tara Montgomery wasn't prone to public displays of affection, but she couldn't help throwing her arms around her longtime boyfriend, Harris Seeman, and squeezing him hard. "I don't want you to go."

"Hey," he said softly, pulling back to look down at her. "You make it seem like I'm moving to another planet."

"Almost." Tara frowned. "California is the other coast."

"Yeah, I know. But we both agreed this was an opportunity I couldn't pass up." Harris released an exhilarated breath. "I still can't believe Harmon Graphics and Software actually wants me to oversee the opening of the new firm in San Francisco. If they like the job I do . . . Man, what if they offer me one of the top positions in the company?"

Harris's smile was contagious, and Tara's own lips curved upward. But with the moment of happiness for her boyfriend also came a moment of doubt. This was the opportunity of a lifetime for him, the culmination of so many years of hard work. If he was indeed offered a top position with Harmon

Graphics & Software, would he ever return to Miami?

"I'll be back once a month," he said in response to her unspoken question. "And you can come and visit me. Don't worry, sweetheart. We're going to make this work."

"I'm so glad to hear you say that." Tara's shoulders drooped with relief. She was being silly, she realized, as Harris rubbed his hands up and down her arms. Just because he was going away for at least six months didn't mean their relationship would suffer. They'd been together for nearly five years.

"Tara?"

"Hmm?" She looked up when she realized she'd drifted off in her thoughts.

A huge grin spread on Harris's face. "Open your hand."

Tara looked up at him with surprise, wondering what he was suddenly up to. And when he reached into his jacket pocket and withdrew a small velvet blue box, her heart danced with excitement.

"C'mon, sweetheart. Open your hand."

"Harris, what—"

"Open."

She did, hardly able to suppress the bubble of excitement in her throat. Harris placed the small ring box in the palm of her hand.

"Oh, goodness, Harris."

"Go ahead," he urged.

The airport passersby slowed to regard her and Harris, who stood approximately twenty feet from the security checkpoints that only passengers with boarding passes could go beyond. Good God, Harris was proposing to her right in the Miami International Airport?

"Sweetheart, I have a plane to catch."

"Yes, yes, of course." Tara blew out a nervous breath as she opened the box. Her chest tightened with the slightest disappointment. Yes, it was beautiful, but this diamond cluster ring certainly couldn't be an engagement ring.

Could it?

Harris took her hand in his. "It's a promise ring," he explained. "We've been together for five years, and I plan to spend my life with you."

"Oh, Harris." He'd never quite come out and said those words before, even though she knew in her heart how he felt about her. "I want to spend my life with you, too."

"With my professional life up in the air right now, I didn't want to make any definite plans yet. Not until things settle down and I know what I'm going to be doing. Then, we can talk about our future."

And whether or not they would continue to live in Miami or on the West Coast. Of course; that made sense.

"But before I left . . ." Harris paused as he looked directly into her eyes. "I wanted there to be no doubt about how I feel about you. So this ring is my promise that I'll always love you. And I want you to be Mrs. Harris Seeman."

The disappointment Tara had felt earlier dissipated with the warmth of Harris's words. Her eyes misted, and a little sob of happiness escaped her. "Oh, Harris. I love you."

"And if I get that promotion I believe I'm going to get, I will be able to buy you any engagement ring your heart desires. *Any* one."

Oh, how Tara loved this man. She had hoped for an official engagement ring, but Harris was practical and would want to do everything right. He would propose when he felt the time was perfect, and he certainly wouldn't do so in an airport. A fine dining establishment would be his style.

Which was fine by her.

"Will you put it on me?" Tara asked.

Harris took the ring box from her hand, took out the ring, then slipped it on the third finger of her right hand. It was a perfect fit.

Tara held her hand out, splaying the fingers to see how her new piece of jewelry looked. It was beautiful.

"Thank you, Harris. Not just for the ring, but for everything it means."

Surprising her, Harris responded by bringing his mouth down on hers and kissing her softly. As he was about to pull away, Tara slipped her arms around his neck and urged him closer, deepening the kiss. Forget what her father had always told her about public displays of affection. This was the man she loved, and she needed to savor his lips on hers because she didn't know when she would see him again.

With a moan of regret, Harris pulled away. "Now, I really have to go." With a finger, he stroked her chin. "But every time you look at that ring, remember my words. Remember my promise."

"I will." Tara pressed her right hand over her chest, a smile forming on her face. "I definitely will."

One

Six months later . . .

"So, which one do you prefer?" Tara gently fingered the silky material samples on the bed beside her, then held them up. "The pale pink, or the mauve?"

The pink was definitely nice, but so was the mauve. But matching flowers might be easier to do if the bridesmaids dresses were pink. "Hmm, Diamond?" Tara prompted.

Her question was met with silence, and no longer absorbed in the moment of planning her happy event, Tara looked across the room at her cousin and best friend. The sparkle in her eyes, for which she'd earned the nickname Diamond years ago, was gone.

Tara instantly realized that something was wrong. She placed the samples on her lap. "Diamond? What is it? What's wrong?"

Diamond let out a weary breath as she raised her eyes to meet her cousin's. "Oh, Tara."

"What?" The tone of her cousin's voice made her back go rigid with fear. "It's not Paul, is it?" Diamond's relationship with her current live-in boyfriend had been more off than on in the past few months.

"No. Paul and I are working things out. Things are cool on that front."

"Okay," Tara said, somewhat warily. "Then what is it?"

"You . . . there's nothing you want to tell me?"

Tara gave Diamond a dumbfounded look. "You're the one who seems to have something to say. Ever since you came over, you've been distant, quiet. It's not because I'm talking about the wedding plans, is it? You're not thinking of Tyrone, are you?"

Diamond dismissed the idea with a wave of the hand. "No, no. I am definitely over Tyrone. I'm better off without him, and can only be thankful we didn't end up walking down the aisle."

"Okay, sweetie. Then I'm confused."

Diamond began pacing the floor beside the bedroom window. "I guess I keep hoping that I'm wrong. That if you haven't heard—"

Tara stood abruptly, and Diamond stopped her pacing. "Please just tell me what's going on," Tara said.

Diamond closed her eyes, as if painfully, then re-opened them. "Sweetie, I wouldn't even mention anything if what I heard didn't come from a reliable source. Harris—" She paused. "Oh, there's no other way to say this than to just say this. Harris is apparently engaged."

For three long seconds, Tara stared at her cousin, trying to digest her words. Finally, she said, "Well, we're not officially engaged, but yes, he's going to marry me."

"From what I heard, he *is* officially engaged—to someone else."

"That's ridiculous," Tara replied quickly. "Where would you have heard such a thing?"

"Tara, no one more than me wishes that what I heard wasn't true. But you know that his sister Melanie works at the radio station. She couldn't wait to tell me that Harris is engaged to someone in San Francisco."

At the mention of Melanie's name, Tara actually chuckled. Well, no wonder Diamond had heard such a story. "I don't think it's a surprise to anyone that Melanie doesn't like me. No doubt she's just trying to stir up trouble."

"That's what I thought. Until she showed me this." Diamond carefully unfolded a piece of newspaper and passed it to Tara.

As Tara looked down at the paper, her hands started to tremble. Surely this headline was wrong. Lord, it had to be.

But it was right there in black and white. "Harris Seeman announces engagement to San Francisco socialite?" Her voice raised in pitch as she finished reading the headline. "What?" She swallowed painfully. "How can this be? We—he said—no, he promised—that we'd get engaged just as soon as he knew what was going on with his life."

"Yeah, well, it seems that Harris forgot about that."

Tara looked down at the clipping, scanning the rest of the announcement. She suddenly felt ill.

"Didn't you tell me you hadn't heard from Harris in a while?"

"Yes, but . . ." Mentally, Tara started to sum up all the clues she hadn't picked up on. Harris had been brief with her the last few times they'd talked. He'd promised to return calls but hadn't. When she'd questioned him about it the last time, he'd apologized and told her that he was so swamped with work, he didn't know when he'd have the time to talk with her at length.

Tara had believed him because . . . well, because she'd had no reason not to. After all, he'd made promises to her that day six months ago at the airport. Promises she'd expected him to keep.

But she was a big girl, and she understood that sometimes things didn't work out. But if Harris had gone to San Francisco and fallen for someone else, why hadn't he been man enough and told her?

No, none of this made sense. "He's only been in San Francisco for six months," Tara said. "Who gets engaged after six months?"

"To be honest, I wouldn't have expected this of Harris—especially since he didn't even suggest marriage to you until you'd been dating for five years. Unless, of course, he was involved with Aisha Harmon while he was involved with you."

"No." Tara's voice was a horrified whisper. There was no way she would believe that. Harris would never do that to her.

But then, did she truly know Harris at all? She scanned the announcement once again. "Harris Seeman and Aisha Harmon proudly announce their engagement. The vice president of Harmon Graphics and Software is to wed the socialite daughter of Lawrence Harmon, founder and CEO of the company, early next year."

Tara couldn't stand any more. She crumpled the newspaper clipping into a ball and tossed it toward the garbage tin. It hit the rim, then fell onto the carpet.

Perfect. Just perfect.

"Sweetie, come here." Diamond wrapped her arms around her shoulders. "I'm sorry. Even sorrier that you had to hear this from me. But if this is true—and it seems very likely that it is—then you're better off without him."

"I don't understand. Why would he do this?" The scene at the airport played out in her mind again, though now instead of pleasure she felt stinging betrayal. "You should have seen him at the airport—so happy. So . . ." Tara's voice trailed off, ending on a sad sigh. "There was no need for that, not if he was already involved with Aisha."

"He's a d-o-g, dog, that's what he is."

"So, Aisha's the boss's daughter." Tara spoke to herself as much as to Diamond. "Maybe that's what this is about. His damn aspirations to climb the corporate ladder."

Diamond squeezed her tighter. "Probably. Which makes him even more of a dog."

Tara's eyes ventured to the scraps of material on the bed. She'd taken it upon herself to informally start planning the wedding, all to make things easier on him when he eventually popped the question. And now she felt like a fool with a capital F.

She covered her face with both hands—then remembered the ring. As she lowered her hand to look at it, Harris's words played in her head: *Every time you look at that ring, remember my words. Remember my promise.*

God, what a joke! What a slap in the face after the five years she'd spent with him, giving him the best she had to offer anyone.

She jerked the ring off her finger and hurled it across the room. It hit the wall hard, no doubt leaving a mark, then dropped to the carpet.

A minute passed before Tara spoke. Her moment of anger was replaced by melancholy. "Should I call him?"

Diamond sucked her teeth in disapproval. "Call him? And make him think you're pining over him? Girl, keep your pride intact. If he's chosen to give you the brush-off, then ignore him. Hell, make him sweat, wondering how easily you may have moved on and what gorgeous man is offering you comfort."

Tara's attempt at a smile failed. Instead, she nodded grimly. Her cousin may have been a couple years younger than she, but she'd had her fair share of experience with men, her fair share of heartbreak. Unfortunately, Tara could learn a thing or two from Diamond Montgomery.

"And if it'll make you feel better, I'll help you torch all his pictures—and anything else that will remind you of him."

Tara couldn't help chuckling. "Just like you did with Tyrone's stuff?" After a whirlwind romance with Tyrone, he and Diamond had become engaged. But when she'd learned that he was still seeing his ex and the mother of his two children on the sly, she'd kicked his cheating butt to the curb in grand style. That was Diamond—always dramatic.

"Girl, you know how much better I felt after that. Burned that man right from my memory and *moved on.*"

"Maybe you're right. Maybe that's exactly what I need to do."

"Except for that ring," Diamond interjected quickly. "That's a very nice ring. You want to take that someplace where you can get a pretty penny for it. Then buy yourself something else you really need."

"Oh, God." Tara laughed. "That's awful."

"And exactly what you deserve."

Tara's laughter suddenly turned to tears. She'd tried so hard to hold her emotions in check, but now they overwhelmed her.

"Come here." Diamond wrapped her in a warm embrace. "It's gonna be okay, Tara. Everything's gonna be all right."

Two

"Oh yes, Sandals is a great spot to go for a honeymoon." Tara spoke the words in a monotone voice, trying her best to put the memory of Harris and his betrayal behind her. But it was nearly impossible, considering that Murphy's law had her dealing with an unusual amount of honeymoon travel since her relationship had fallen apart—or was it simply that she noticed it more now, given her situation?

It was even more of a painful reminder because she and Harris had planned to honeymoon at one of the Sandals resorts.

Suppressing a sigh, Tara glanced at the colorful Sandals poster that sat on one corner of her desk. A happy couple, embracing lovingly, against a gorgeous Caribbean backdrop—what could be more ideal? Uncharacteristic of most travel destinations, the resort actually looked better than the pictures—at least the ones she'd seen when she'd visited as a travel agent.

"Which island would you recommend?" The woman seated across the desk from her spoke in a voice bubbling with excitement. Yes, Tara realized, this woman's whole body oozed it.

And why shouldn't she be excited? She was about to marry the man she loved.

I wonder if he'll dump you before you head down the aisle. . . .

"We were thinking St. Lucia." The woman clutched her fiancé's hand as she gazed into his eyes and grinned. She turned back to Tara. "Of course, Jamaica has six different Sandals resorts to choose from. Isn't it true that if you stay at one, you can play at all?"

"You've done your homework."

"Gosh, Steven." The woman bit down on her lip. "Decisions, decisions."

"Any one you pick will be fine," Tara said, sounding as if she were trying to sell coffins, not a wonderful honeymoon package. Man, she had to snap out of this funk!

"You don't seem so sure," Steven said warily.

"I don't?" Tara tried to force a smile, but knew she failed. It had been two weeks since she'd learned that Harris was marrying someone else. She wondered where he would take the boss's daughter for a honeymoon. Sandals, or an exclusive island somewhere that only the rich and famous frequented?

"Miss?"

"I'm so sorry," Tara said quickly. "I'm . . . I'm having a bad day. My focus isn't what it should be." This time, she managed a genuine smile. "Let's start over."

The happy couple perked up. Tara went through the impressive list of features that the Sandals resorts had to offer to honeymooning couples.

"So," she said, in closing, "since they're all couples-only resorts, they all have the same romantic amenities and features. Any one you go to will give you fabulous dining, private outdoor hot tubs nestled in beautiful island gardens, a variety of water sports, golf. Everything you can imagine is included. So, you just have to decide—do you want a more quaint island or do you want to do some exploring? St. Lucia is smaller, and there are only two Sandals resorts on the island that you could explore. As for Jamaica, it's a bigger island, with six Sandals resorts. There are three in the Montego Bay area, two in Ocho Rios, and one in Negril. While you can play at any of the island's Sandals resorts if you're staying at one, only the ones in the same areas offer free shuttles to and from its various resorts. You can easily take the Air Jamaica Express if you want to travel to different parts of the island, but that's going to cost more. I guess the best bang for your buck, if you want to go to more than one of the resorts, is to choose one in Montego Bay. Did I mention that Sandals Royal Caribbean has a private offshore island?"

"You're kidding?" the woman said, but her eyes lit up like beacons.

"Not at all." Tara grabbed one of the brochures that featured the Jamaican Sandals, and opened to a page that displayed the offshore island at the resort in Montego Bay. She showed it to the couple. "Here it is. The private island has a pool with a swim-up pool bar, a fabulous Indonesian restaurant. And the beach is *very* private."

"That sounds heavenly."

"And the resort also has a butler service. They all do, depending on which suite you choose."

The bride and groom-to-be turned to each other and began discussing the option of booking a suite, to get the butler service. "It's our honeymoon," the woman said. "Why not pamper ourselves?"

They turned back to Tara, beaming, but then confusion passed over both their faces.

Tara chuckled. "I know. Decisions, decisions. I could sell you on any one of these resorts and you'd be extremely happy. But—and I don't mean to make your decision more difficult—you might want to consider Sandals Dunn's River in the Ocho Rios area. It is absolutely stunning. And if you've never been to Jamaica before, you might be interested in the Ocho Rios area because that's where you'll find Dunn's River Falls. It's one of the island's biggest attractions."

"The big waterfall that everyone climbs?" Steven asked.

"Yep."

"What do you think, Amy?"

"We can't go to Jamaica and not climb Dunn's River Falls. It's probably easier to be in that area."

"That's what I was thinking." Steven smiled, then planted a soft kiss on his fiancée's lips.

Again, Tara couldn't help remembering Harris, couldn't help remembering how happy he'd made her the day he left for San Francisco. The couple before her was the epitome of happiness—at least right now. She hoped they stayed that way forever.

Tara flipped the Sandals brochure to the section that boasted the Dunn's River location. "Believe me, this resort is stunning. You'll have a fabulous honeymoon—a great way to start a marriage."

Tara was close to sealing the deal, and the mention of the butler service had the couple considering a suite rather than a regular room. Judging by the rock on Amy's finger, Steven would pay any price to make her happy.

Up-sell. The word sounded in her mind. Tara doubted it would be hard to persuade them to book a suite. The higher the sale, the more commission she made. Sandals was not an inexpensive resort.

"Now," she said, pushing the bad memories of Harris from her mind so she could concentrate on her job, "let me tell you about their expansive suites. . . ."

Tara stood, stretched, then glanced at the wall clock in the back of the office. Eleven-seventeen A.M. The morning was dragging on. After Amy and Steven had left, it had been fairly slow in the office, and she wished it were at least noon so she could take her break.

Tara worked in a small but well-established travel agency in downtown Miami, which was exactly what she liked. When she'd first started out in the travel business after college, she had worked for a couple of large agencies, only to learn quickly that there you were just a small fish in a big pond, and if your sales weren't what the company expected, you wouldn't last long. She had lasted, but she had never been rewarded for her efforts. She should have gotten a promotion and a raise, but neither came. She'd quit the first agency and gone to another reputable one, only to find that their commission breakdowns and payments were shady.

Both negative experiences had left her with a bad taste in her mouth. Then, she'd found Wholesale Travel. She'd been with them now for the past four years and she was very happy.

Tara strolled to the nearby water cooler, glancing at the picturesque travel posters around the office: a breathtaking view of the Rocky Mountains; an idyllic island sunset in Barbados; a Royal Caribbean cruise liner sailing through a deep, blue ocean; and of course, the huge promotional poster for the chain of Sandals resorts.

"Great job, Tara." David, who was the sole occupant of the product department at this location, gave her a bright smile on his way from the watercooler.

"Thanks," she replied. Steven and Amy had not been like some customers who tried to scrimp and save every penny possible, leaving an agent with a next-to-nil profit, all to keep the customer happy. Steven had the money to spend on a fabulous vacation, and he spent it—no questions asked.

"That guy must love her."

"No doubt." Tara reached for a paper cup. She liked working here. None of her colleagues copped an attitude about anything, and they weren't cutthroat and back-stabbing like some of the people she'd worked with at the two larger companies. David, Sarah, Janice, Sharnette, and Barry were like family. Going to work was a pleasure.

And unlike the first two companies where she'd worked, she was actually moving up the ladder here. She was now senior travel consultant, and with that title had come a salary, full benefits, stock options, and raises every year.

There were three Wholesale Travel locations in South Florida, and a couple dozen across the country. The head office was in West Palm Beach, and they handled all administrative matters, such as company advertising, IATA issues, and payroll. Tara had started at the Fort Lauderdale location, and with her last promotion over a year ago, she had been sent to the location in downtown Miami. This was better for her as it was closer to home, anyway.

As senior travel consultant, she had the most seniority of the travel agents, and along with the manager, pretty much ran this location. She dealt with all the matters in the front of the shop; Barry dealt with all the money matters and reported to the head office. Tara's life had been going according to plan. After being senior travel consultant for three years would come the opportunity to buy more company stock—and actually own a decent share of the company. This had been her plan. With total job security and marriage to Harris, she had planned to start a family in the next few years. She'd wanted it all: the beautiful house with the white picket fence and the two-point-five children.

Well, she would have settled for two. Hopefully a boy and a girl. But now, Harris had put a wrench in those plans.

Harris. She sighed. She would do well to put him out of her mind once and for all. The lying louse hadn't even had the decency to call and speak to her after announcing his engagement to the world. He'd called her home while she was at work and left a message saying that he was sorry about everything but was following his heart and hoped that she understood.

She hadn't called him back.

And while her brain knew that she should forget him, she couldn't quite erase him from her heart.

"Hey, Tara. You okay?"

Tara whirled around, surprised to see Sharnette standing beside her. Sharnette was the receptionist, but she was also responsible for the office's ticketing as they were too small to have a ticketing department. She made sure that all tickets were mailed or couriered to their customers.

"Yeah. Yeah. I'm fine."

"You did well with that last sale," Sharnette said in an effort to buoy her spirits. She filled a paper cup with water, then drank it.

"In the end." Tara had sold the couple on one of the best suites at Sandals Dunn's River. It had cost them a pretty penny, and she'd earned a very nice commission on the package deal.

"Don't be so hard on yourself. After all you've been through, it's no wonder you're not in the mood to sell honeymoon packages. I give you credit for even coming in to work at all."

"It's been two weeks, Sharnette."

"Two weeks to try and let go of someone you loved for five years *and* deal with the way he ended things?"

The door chimes sang, indicating that someone had arrived, and Tara was thankful for the diversion. No matter how well-meaning everyone was, it didn't help for them to keep treating her as if she were an emotional cripple.

"Hmm."

The pique in Sharnette's voice made Tara face the door.

"Now he is *fine,*" Sharnette went on. She gave Tara a sly look. "Guess you've got work to do."

"No, Sharnette." Tara felt a spurt of panic, and she wasn't sure why. "I don't want to . . . I was going to head out for lunch."

"But I'm heading out for lunch right now, which means Sarah is going to take over my desk until I'm back. And Janice is busy." Sharnette gave her a sweet smile. "You're not afraid of dealing with this sinfully fine gentleman, are you?"

"Sharnette, just find out what he's interested in and give him some brochures—"

But Sharnette was already crossing the office to her desk. Tara watched her grab her purse.

Tara quickly shot a glance in Janice's direction. Janice was still on the phone, immersed in conversation.

As Sharnette made her way past the handsome gentleman, Tara heard her say, "Tara Montgomery will be pleased to help you, sir." Then, behind the man's head, Sharnette offered Tara a bright but mischievous smile.

The man met her eyes, and Tara forced a grin.

She would get her friend for this.

Three

No doubt about it, he *was* fine.

Tara couldn't help noticing the attractive features of his face. The sexy and very kissable full lips. The deep-set light brown eyes. The adorable dimples.

And one killer smile.

Her heart actually fluttered when he curled his lips in one of those smiles and started toward her.

"You're Tara?" he asked.

Tara smoothed a hand over her long, floral skirt. "Yes."

"Nice to meet you." He extended a hand, and Tara shook it. "I'm Darren Burkeen."

"Hello, Darren. My desk is right this way. Let's have a seat there." Tara led the way to her desk, where she sank into her chair. Darren sat opposite her.

She folded her hands on top of her desk in a professional gesture. "What can I help you with today?"

"I'm actually here to inquire about cruise packages. Something cozy and romantic, yet exciting."

Not another couple-related trip. Why couldn't this man be here to take a solitary vacation across Europe?

"Is this for a honeymoon?" Tara asked.

"Oh, no." Darren shook his head to quash that idea. "I'm actually thinking of surprising my parents with a trip for their fortieth wedding anniversary."

"Oh," Tara crooned, relaxing a little. "That's so sweet."

"I figure they deserve it. They've worked hard all their lives and now's the time for them to kick back and relax a little. But have some fun at the same time."

"That is one of the nicest things I've heard in a long time," Tara commented, and meant it. Mostly, people came in to book trips for themselves. Sometimes parents inquired about vacations for their children, such as honeymoon packages, but Tara couldn't remember ever having dealt with someone who had come in to purchase a vacation for his parents.

"When's their anniversary?"

"In four months."

"Four months?" Tara couldn't hide her surprise.

"I figured I'd get a head start on planning something. See how viable an option it is."

"And this is going to be a surprise?"

"Yes."

"Hmm." Tara sounded doubtful. "Forty years together is quite the landmark. What if they're already planning something special?"

"That's one of the reasons I'm looking into it now. But I've already been asking some questions, and I think that as much as my father would love to take my mother on a vacation to celebrate, he's concerned about money. He retired a couple months back, so they're watching the budget."

"Understandable."

"Yeah." Darren nodded. "So, it'd be really nice to be able to do this for them."

Darren's soft smile reached his eyes, and once again, Tara couldn't help noticing how handsome he was. But more importantly, he certainly seemed like a decent man. Any man who would think of surprising his parents with a cruise for their anniversary couldn't be a louse.

It was nice to know that there were a few decent ones left out there. If Darren had a wife or girlfriend, she was no doubt a lucky woman.

"Any particular type of cruise you had in mind? Caribbean, Mediterranean? Or how about—" Tara stopped talking, startled when she noticed that Darren was staring at her intently, so intently that he didn't seem to hear her question. She shifted uncomfortably in her seat. "Um, Darren?"

"I'm sorry. What were you saying?"

Tara shifted in her seat, then replied, "I asked if you had a specific type of cruise in mind, such as Caribbean or Mediterranean."

He didn't answer right away, and Tara waited for him to speak.

After several long seconds, he said, "I'm sorry if I'm not quite paying attention. It's just that you have the most amazing eyes."

"Excuse me?" Tara's tone relayed her surprise.

There was that killer smile again. "Your eyes. I can't help it—they're distracting me from what you're saying."

Tara felt a sudden surge of annoyance. Until this moment, Darren had seemed like a very nice man, a respectable one, different from the average man she dealt with. She was disappointed to hear some tired line coming from his mouth. "If you don't

Kayla Perrin

mind," Tara said bluntly, "I'd like to keep our dealings strictly business."

Darren paused, then said, "Yes, of course. I'm sorry. I didn't mean to offend you."

Darren sounded genuinely contrite, and Tara couldn't help feeling that she'd been too hard on him. Quite frankly, had it not been for the whole fiasco with Harris, she would have taken Darren's compliment as nothing more serious than playful flirting. She might even have been a little flattered. But the truth was, these days, she had a hard time thinking anything positive about any member of the opposite sex.

"No offense taken," Tara assured him. "It's been one of those days, ya know?"

Darren gave a slight nod.

"All right," Tara began, getting back down to business. "Since you're not sure yet which cruise you might be interested in purchasing, why don't I give you some brochures that you can take with you and look over? If you have any questions, please call me. And of course, please call me when you're ready to book a package."

Tara handed Darren the brochures, and he rolled them into a tube shape after accepting them. "Thanks a lot," he said. "I will definitely be back."

Standing, Tara gave Darren a warm smile. "I look forward to hearing from you."

Darren turned, and Tara's eyes swept over his tall frame. She'd guess him to be around six feet one. He was definitely handsome, and his body was in great shape. She watched him open the door and walk outside.

He didn't turn back for a final glance.

Just as well, Tara thought, sinking back into her chair.

When Tara stood and slipped her purse over her shoulder, Sharnette quickly threw off her telephone headset and jumped up. Before Tara made it to the door, Sharnette was in her path.

"So?" Sharnette said. "You're not going to tell me how it went?"

Tara gave Sharnette a deadpan look, though she knew what her friend was alluding to. "Went with what?"

"With Mr. Too Fine. The hottie."

"Oh." Tara waved a dismissive hand. "I think I should be able to sell him a cruise for—"

"That's not what I mean," Sharnette whined. "Did you get his number, make plans to hook up? You know."

"No, I don't know." Tara gave her a pointed look. "Sharnette, he was a customer, that's all."

"Really?"

"Yes, really."

"And that's why you were so afraid to deal with him?"

"I wasn't afraid."

"Whatever. The point is, you know there were sparks between you two." She paused, then added, "You know what you need to do, even if you're gonna deny it."

A comeback had already formed in her mind, but Tara kept it in check. She was not interested in having a debate with Sharnette, because Sharnette's solutions always had to do with sex.

"I know I need to go for lunch." Tara stepped past Sharnette and reached for the door.

"You need a good old-fashioned palette cleanser."

Tara's hand paused. "A *what?*"

"Don't even play like you don't know what I mean. I was thinking about it over lunch, and I'm more convinced of the solution by the minute."

"I'm not sure I want to hear this."

"You've been in such a slump, and I totally understand." Sharnette placed an arm across Tara's shoulders. "You and Harris were an item for five years. You're still hurting over him, which is understandable, but because of the seriousness of your relationship, you have to do something equally as serious to get him out of your system."

"Sharnette—"

"The best thing you can do to get over him is get involved with someone else. Physically."

Tara rolled her eyes. "Girl, you are too much."

"That's what I did after you know who—and it made a world of difference for me. On the nights I missed him, I remembered my newer experience, and it helped to erase the old from my mind."

"Girl, you are crazy."

"Trust me, it works. The key is to make sure it's just a physical thing—no emotional involvement whatsoever. Let's face it. That customer was hot. If you're gonna have a palette cleanser, I can't imagine a guy who'd be easier to get in the mood with."

Laughing, Tara shrugged out from under Sharnette's arm. "Get out of my way."

"Think about it," Sharnette called after her.

Not in this lifetime, Tara replied silently.

Finally out of the office, Tara turned left, heading to the burger joint a few doors away. She needed calories, and she needed them quickly, before she passed out.

She opened the door to the restaurant and stepped inside. The smell of hamburgers on the grill wafted into her nose, making her stomach grumble in anticipation.

Then her stomach dropped to her knees in shock.

Darren!

His face lit up as he saw her, and a little jolt hit her heart.

"You're following me," Darren said as he strolled toward her, the curve of his lips emphasizing his playful tone.

"No." Tara did her best to be nonchalant. "Just hungry."

"I wish I'd known you were getting a bite to eat. I would have invited you for lunch."

"That wouldn't have been necessary. But thanks anyway."

Darren flicked his wrist forward and looked at his watch. "I've got to be getting back to work."

"Mmm-hmm." Tara deliberately kept her words to a minimum, not wanting to encourage any conversation. Darren seemed nice enough, but she was in no way ready even to think of getting to know him.

"Well, I'll be going."

Tara stopped perusing the menu behind the counter and faced him. Butterflies danced in her stomach at his intense look. Goodness, why did he have to look at her that way? As if he were trying to see into her very soul?

Tara glanced away to break the intensity, then

looked back at him. "I hope to hear from you when you've looked over the brochures."

"Definitely."

"All right. Have a good day."

"I will now."

Tara ignored Darren's suggestive comment. After a moment, he turned to leave, and Tara faced the giant menu once again. A burger was what she wanted. A big, fat, juicy burger, smothered with mozzarella cheese.

"Hello, Tara," Hilda greeted her from behind the counter. "What can I get for you today?"

Tara stepped up to the counter. "Afternoon, Hilda. I'm gonna have one of your burgers. Medium. Onions, relish, mustard, ketchup, and lots of mozzarella cheese."

"You got it."

"I'll take french fries and a lemonade as well."

"No problem. You want to pay for that now, or wait until the order is ready?"

"I'll pay for it now." Tara settled the bill, and Hilda gave her the lemonade. Drink in hand, Tara turned to head to a table.

She nearly had heart failure when she saw Darren was standing at the far corner of the restaurant, near the door.

All right. This definitely wasn't good!

Why hadn't he left yet?

As usual, he gave her a smile, a smile that melted her annoyance. She made her way to a table and sat, even though she saw him approaching.

Darren held up a hand immediately as he neared her. "I know . . . pretty soon you're going to have me up on stalking charges. I really don't mean to be harassing you, but I find you very intriguing, and I'd like to get to know you better."

Intriguing? Tara had never heard that one before.

"I would love to take you out to dinner some time, or a movie. Whatever you'd like."

"Darren, I'm flattered—"

"Then say yes."

Tara stared up at him, and felt bad for what she was about to say. She didn't want to hurt the man's feelings, but this wasn't the right time in her life for dating. She wasn't the least bit interested in getting to know any members of the opposite sex.

"I'm sorry. I'm just . . . It's not personal. I'm sorry."

Darren shrugged nonchalantly. "I guess you can't blame a guy for trying."

"Like I said, I'm flattered. As for the cruise packages, I'll check around and see what type of deals are out there. You can give me a call in a few days for an update."

"Thanks." Darren's eyes now held a hint of disappointment. "I'll talk to you later, then."

"Bye."

This time, Tara watched Darren walk to the door, watched him leave. Why should she feel a smidgen of guilt? She'd told the truth. She wasn't ready to think about dating again, and to lie to herself would be worse.

Worse for both of them.

Nothing good could come of rushing into a new relationship, no matter what Sharnette might say about cleansing her palette. Tara hadn't seen Harris since he'd visited her four months ago, and she'd almost forgotten what sex was.

She didn't miss it. She didn't need it.

And if the urge to get physical with a guy ever came, she'd find someone other than Darren. Already, it was easy to tell that Darren was the relationship kind.

Tara took a sip of her lemonade, but didn't enjoy it. She was too preoccupied with her thoughts.

Yes, Darren was charming. Yes, he was gorgeous.

Unfortunately, Tara had learned that no matter how attractive the package, that didn't guarantee a guy was a good catch.

Four

"That's right, ladies. This is your forum tonight. What's your gripe with your man? Is he spending too much time with the boys? Do you think he's creeping with another woman? Call me. Share with me what's going on in your life.

"This is Lady D, and I'm your host for the *Love Chronicles* on Talk 93, South Florida's hottest talk radio. You can reach me at 555-2100 in Dade county, 555-7455 in Broward, and 555-3860 in Palm Beach county.

"The phone lines are already lighting up, so I know this is a hot topic. We all need a forum to express ourselves, our concerns. I try to do that every night from ten-thirty to midnight here on 93.1 on your FM dial. Now, let me go to my first caller." Diamond read the name of the caller on the screen, then pressed the green button. "I have Christine from Fort Lauderdale on the line."

"Hey, Lady D," Christine began. "I love your show."

"Thank you, sister. What's your gripe tonight?"

"I work three jobs, and every time I come home, I find my man sitting on the sofa, watching TV. The house is a mess, and he expects me to be the one to clean it up, even after I've come home from a long day at work."

"Girl, tell me you're not putting up with that."

"I know, I know. But I'm tired of it. At first, he at least used to do a few things around the house. His big argument was that he took care of our daughter. But now she's in school—and he's doing less and less. Worse, he has every excuse in the book for not getting a job."

"You know you need to kick that man to the curb."

"I've done that before, and every time I do, he comes crying back."

"He can't come back if you don't take him back."

"I know . . ."

"The sex must be something hot, hmm?" Diamond asked, then chuckled.

"Yeah," Christine replied, a smile in her voice. "It is."

"But, girl, you know that no matter how nice the sex is, it ain't gonna pay the bills."

"That's true."

"And obviously he wants to be with you as much as you want to be with him."

"He says he loves me."

"Then this time you give him an ultimatum and mean it. Tell him that you're tired of being the man in the relationship, and that if he doesn't do his part, you're going to walk away and not look back. And, Christine?"

"Yeah?"

"The key to any ultimatum is doing what you say you will if he doesn't keep up his end of the bargain. No matter what—don't cave in when you're horny, or lonely, or when he gives you the same song and dance he always gives you. Stand firm, my sister. And if he really loves you, he's gonna do right by you. So don't you worry about that. And if he doesn't do right by you . . . well, be thankful you didn't waste more time with him."

"Thank you, Lady D. I'm gonna take your advice."

"You're welcome, Christine. And I hope you do take my advice, because you know Lady D would never steer you wrong." Diamond hit the disconnect button, then said, "Now, ladies, I know you like to call me and tell me about your problems and ask my opinion about what you should do. Sometimes what I tell you isn't what you all want to hear, but I guarantee you, I'm giving you good advice. I've dealt with enough brothers—good and bad—to know how they think. They'll always walk over you if you stretch yourself out like a carpet. So do me a favor . . . if you're not really ready to hear what I'm gonna tell you, don't bother calling." Diamond chuckled to soften her words. She pressed another flashing green button. "All right, I have Leslie from Boca on the line. Leslie, how you doing?"

"Hello, Lady D. I'm pretty good."

"Excellent."

"I just want to say I love your show."

"Thank you."

"I have a general comment."

"Speak to me, sister."

"I am just plain *tired* of younger men."

"What you mean, younger? You robbing the cradle?" Diamond laughed.

"No, I mean men my age. Adult men who are supposed to act like adults, but they really act like boys."

"Okay, sister. I hear that."

"I was married to a guy a couple years older than me. He was fine, let me tell you, but he thought that because the Lord had blessed him with good looks, that made him too special to be faithful. He cheated on me twice—that I knew of."

"I take it you're not married anymore?"

"Hell no. He begged me to forgive him the first time, which I did. I figured everyone can make a mistake. But I didn't feel right about it. I didn't completely trust him. Then one of his coworkers called me and told me she'd been seeing him behind my back and she thought I should know."

"Oh no, girl. Ladies"—Diamond spoke emphatically—"why do you knowingly sleep with another woman's man? That is what is wrong with this world. Where's our sisterly bond?" Diamond groaned. "Okay, sister. Go on."

"I left him. And I thought I'd never get married again. But one day at the bar where I work, an older man came in. He's significantly older—"

"How much older?"

"Thirty-seven years."

"Hold up. Did I hear you right? *Thirty-seven* years?"

"Yes."

"And how old are you?"

"Twenty-eight."

"Girl . . . Okay, I've picked up my jaw off the floor. Continue."

"He may be sixty-five, but he's in great shape. Still works out. He's still fine."

"Sister, I'm not trying to dog you, nor judge you for that matter, but you married this man?"

"Yes."

"For love?" Diamond couldn't hide her skepticism.

"Yes, I love him. And I know a lot of your callers may think I married him for money, but it's not like that. He's not a sugar daddy."

"Okay."

"But this was about respect. He knew how to treat a lady, not like these younger men."

"Hey, he's from a different generation."

"True, and I found I like that. He loves me, he takes care of me, and most important of all, he respects me. He would never cheat on me."

"I'm sure you're more than enough woman for him, my sister."

Leslie laughed softly. "I guess I am. But whatever the reason, I like knowing that I don't have to wonder where my man has been when we're apart."

"Some valid points, Leslie. Thanks for the call."

"Thanks, Lady D."

Diamond hit the disconnect button. "Well, you heard Leslie. She's found the solution in an older man. Truthfully, I don't want to feel that we all get so fed up with younger men that we turn to older ones—but to each his own. The truth is—and I know I speak for all women—I'd like to see younger men grow up. Is that too much to expect? Let me ask Ken from Miami. Ken, you're on the line."

"Hello, Lady D."

"Hello, my brother."

"Lady D, I do love listening to you, but I have to say, I don't like how you're doggin' out men tonight."

"I hear you, Ken, but there'd be no dogging if you all didn't disrespect women. True or false?" Diamond loved to be controversial, and to do that, she had to be provocative. Sometimes, she'd provoke an argument, or play devil's advocate to get people's blood boiling. Controversial was what kept people listening to her show. Controversial was what kept her ratings high.

"Oh, come on, Lady D. Now you're painting all men with the same brush."

"No, that's not what I said. In fact, I'm not saying *you're* a bad guy. The fact that you're calling my show makes me inclined to think you're one of the good ones." She laughed. "But while there are certainly some good men out there, too many aren't. *Are* you one of the good ones, Ken? And if so, maybe you have some advice to impart to your fellow brothers?"

Ken didn't respond after a couple of seconds, and Diamond hit the disconnect button, not wanting any dead air. "I guess Ken wasn't one of the good guys, or he'd have some wisdom to impart." Looking at the screen, she picked the next male caller and said, "Maybe Steve from Lauderhill can answer that question. Are you one of the good guys, Steve, and if so, any advice to give?"

"You got what you deserved. Watch your back, Diamond."

Diamond's back went rigid. Instantly, she hit the disconnect button and the dump button, so the quick comment would be edited out of the show. Then she glanced at Rick, her producer, in the booth next to her. He met her gaze with a concerned look.

"Steve?" Diamond asked, knowing full well he couldn't respond. "Ooops," she continued. "It seems we've lost Steve. Sorry, Steve. The universe must be telling me this is a night just for the ladies.

"So, ladies—what's your gripe tonight? Let me know what you don't like about the man—or men—

in your lives." Diamond repeated the various phone numbers for the three counties. "I'll continue taking your calls after this commercial break."

Diamond hit the white button to start the commercial, then took off her headphones and dropped them on the stool next to her. She climbed off her own stool and headed for the door. Rick was already out of the booth. He'd left his intern, Claudia, in the booth loading the commercial, news, and weather carts that would play during the next break.

"I'm sorry, Diamond," Rick said as she swung the door open.

Diamond wasn't concerned about the weird call itself; she often got them. It was part of doing talk radio. You were bound to upset some people. "Is my mind playing tricks on me because of the hour, or did Steve just call me by my name?"

"He called you Diamond."

Diamond bit down on her bottom lip, baffled. There might be a handful of callers who knew her real name, but everyone addressed her by her stage name, Lady D.

Everyone except Clay.

Diamond's stomach tightened with fear, though the thought of Clay shouldn't scare her. The crazy man who'd made her life a living hell for months was locked up.

She asked, "There haven't been any strange calls to the station, have there, Rick?"

"Nothing I know of. And if I did, you know I'd tell you."

"Yeah, I'm sure you would." Diamond crossed her arms over her chest and bit down on her lip.

"Why, has someone been harassing you?"

She shook her head. "No. But I guess with a call like that, I can't help remembering Clay."

"Clay can't hurt you where he is."

"Yes, I know that."

"One-minute warning, Diamond."

Diamond went back into her studio, slipped her headphones on again, then sat in front of the microphone. She watched Rick in the booth as he gave her the ten-second countdown with his fingers.

Five. Four. Three. Two. One.

"This is Lady D, and I'm your host for *The Love Chronicles* on Talk 93, South Florida's hottest talk radio. Tonight is your night, ladies. What's your gripe with your man?"

Diamond continued her spiel, but she couldn't stop thinking about the last call and what it meant.

She couldn't help wondering, was it starting again?

Later, Diamond lay in bed with Paul, her arm around him, his arm around her. They lay face-to-face. It was the kind of night for intimate snuggling and talking, then falling asleep in the comfort of each other's arms.

Paul had filled her in on his day at the Hollywood Police Department, and she'd just finished telling him about her strange caller.

"At least the rest of the night went smoothly," Diamond continued. "But the call kind of freaked me out. I don't know why . . . I guess it reminded me of Clay."

Paul had been stroking her back with his fingers, but his hand now stilled. "You need to stop doing that radio show."

"What?"

"You heard me, Diamond. I know I've mentioned this before, but now I think you really ought to listen. Stop doing the show."

"Is that an order?"

"It's a strong suggestion. A wise one."

Diamond pulled out of his arms and rolled over, giving him her back. "That's not an option, Paul."

"Then tone down your show. Do something other than the controversial topics you love so much."

"I'm not going to live my life in fear. This is what I do best. People love the controversy. That's how I became popular."

There were several seconds of silence. Then Paul said, "Fine—you don't want to give up your precious popularity. What about me?"

"What's that supposed to mean? You're gonna leave me if I don't stop doing the show?"

"That's not what I said."

"Then what are you saying?"

"I wonder if you care about me at all, about what matters to me."

"This isn't about you," Diamond replied testily. "I worked in radio before you, and I'm not about to stop doing what I love."

"That's where you're wrong. This is about us, about your safety, and that affects me. It's bad enough that you leave the station so late at night."

"You want me to give up everything I've worked hard to achieve because some idiot calls me?"

"If you thought it was simply some idiot, you wouldn't have mentioned it."

"I mentioned it because it was something that happened during my day, that's all. I didn't expect you to overreact."

"Sure. Now you think it was an innocent call."

"It just shook me up, that's all."

Diamond didn't know what to say. Neither did Paul, judging by the tension-filled silence.

But after a minute, Paul's arm crept around Diamond's waist. "I love you, Diamond. You have to know that. You might think I'm overreacting, but that's where this concern stems from."

"I know—"

"You went through hell when that psycho Clay came after you. He almost killed you. Do you really want to go through that again?"

"Of course not."

"Then you can't keep doing what you're doing."

"Paul . . ."

"No, hear me out. Your newspaper column was very popular. If you go back to doing that, you can still give people the same advice. And at least if guys aren't hearing your sultry voice over the radio, they'll be more likely to leave you alone."

Diamond's back stiffened. "So this is my fault?"

"I'm not saying that," Paul quickly replied. "But right now, you're like a carrot being dangled in front of a horse's mouth. They can't help but bite."

"There haven't been any problems since Clay, and that was two years ago. I'm hardly a carrot."

"And how many letters from guys do you get all the time, telling you how much they want to date you?"

"Letters are harmless."

"Clay started sending letters. He graduated to calling. Then physically stalking you."

"Are you *trying* to scare me?"

"I'm trying to make you understand how serious

this is. You were lucky the first time. Why play Russian roulette with your life?"

In response, Diamond sighed. "You're a cop, Paul. You see the worst side of every situation."

"That's because I've often been called to the scene when some guy's beaten his wife, or some woman's ex can't let her go and he's hacked her to pieces."

"This really isn't helping—"

"No, you need to hear this. I am afraid for you."

"I'll be extra careful. Have the station personnel look out for anything suspicious."

"Yeah, and when someone like Clay gets ahold of you again, what good will that do? The problem is that anyone knows where to go to find you. At least when you worked only for the paper, you could do that from anywhere. People might be able to find you at work, but it's much less likely that they'll find you where you live. Think about this—Clay waited for you outside the radio station. He followed you around. He left notes for you on your car. Ultimately, he tried to abduct you—after which, who knows what he would have done?"

"I know what he did." It had unnerved Diamond to receive calls from Clay, telling her he'd seen her at one of the radio station's events, and that he'd liked what she was wearing that day, or whatever bizarre thing he decided to tell her. He'd made a point of letting her know that he'd seen her, regardless of whether she'd been aware of it. He'd wanted her to feel fear, and she had.

"The radio announces your public events—anyone who wants to get to you can. You're like a sitting duck."

"Paul, it's late. I don't want to talk about this anymore."

"You should at least consider getting a gun."

"Paul." Diamond hated the idea of guns. It was bad enough that Paul brought his home from work.

"Fine. I don't know why I bother. My opinion means nothing to you."

Diamond didn't respond, and after a moment, Paul grunted and took his hand from her body. He rolled over, pulling much of the sheets with him. His back now faced her back.

Great, Diamond thought. So much for a nice night of cuddling. She didn't bother to try and fight for the sheets. She was tired of battling with Paul.

Placing her hand under her pillow for more leverage, she sighed. Part of her ached to turn to Paul and wrap her arms around him, but the other part of her was angry that he didn't understand her position.

Why should *she* have to give up all she'd worked for in her career, just because a few men out there were idiots?

She should have known better. Paul was a chronic worrier. She'd hoped for some comfort in her time of unease, because the call had unnerved her more than she wanted to admit. Instead, Paul had made her feel even worse with his vision of how horribly things could end.

Next time, she would know better and keep minor events like this to herself.

And she certainly wouldn't bother Paul with her nagging fear that something bad was about to happen.

Five

"I'm sure it was probably an isolated incident," Tara said into her headset, trying to offer Diamond reassurance. "But after the last time, you know you obviously have to watch the situation, and if there's even a hint of a more serious problem, take action."

"Yeah, I know. I'm sure it's nothing."

Despite her words, Diamond didn't sound so certain. "Nothing more has happened, has it?"

"No, no. Nothing. It's just that . . ."

Tara sat up straighter at her desk. "What?"

"I don't know why, but I've been having some nightmares lately. Nightmares about Clay."

"Clay? Why?"

"Hell if I know. He's locked up, so I know he can't hurt me. I don't know why."

"You want to come over later? Maybe we can head out for dinner or something."

"Yeah, that sounds nice. I'm not sure I want to see Paul before I head off to work anyway."

"You two are fighting?"

"Paul wants me to quit the show."

"Because of this?"

"He's never liked me doing it anyway, especially because we work different hours and hardly see

each other, but yeah, now he's using this call to try
and persuade me to quit."

"You're not going to do that, are you?" It was a
question, but Tara was certain of the answer. There
was no way her feisty cousin was going to let anyone
scare her out of doing what she loved.

"No." Diamond paused. "It's not like he makes
a suggestion, nor like he understands what he's really asking of me. He thinks I'm simply supposed to
listen to him, because he's a cop, and he knows best.
Well, it'll be a cold day in hell before I give up my
career. It's a career I had before I met him. You
know how hard I worked to get where I'm at."

Tara did know. At twenty-seven, Diamond had
worked hard as a journalist and now had a success-
ful radio show in which she gave advice to callers
about various problems in their relationships. She'd
started off writing a column for her college paper
on the subject of relationships years earlier, had
graduated and gotten work for a small magazine in
South Florida, and ultimately a regular column with
the *Sun Sentinel.* Her no-nonsense, straight-to-the-
point advice had garnered her attention in all of
South Florida, and guest radio spots had followed.
Ultimately, Talk 93, South Florida's most popular
talk radio station, had offered her a regular spot in
addition to her work at the *Sun Sentinel.* She'd
stopped doing the column when her radio show had
quickly become a hit.

Now, Diamond was enjoying success and recogni-
tion, but that very success was often threatening to
the men she dated.

"I can understand that he's worried," Tara said,
"especially after the whole nightmare with Clay."

Clay had been an obsessed fan, who'd started off

writing Diamond graphic letters about what he wanted to do to her sexually. From there, he had progressed to calling her. Then stalking. Letters were left on her car. Roses. Gifts. All items Diamond had no interest in.

Then, one day as Diamond had entered the office of Talk 93, Clay had snuck up behind her and attempted to drag her to a waiting car. Two men had seen Diamond's plight and gone to her aid. They'd successfully freed Diamond and apprehended Clay. He was arrested, and was currently serving time in a facility for the criminally insane.

"I know. But Paul overreacted. He went on and on about how I'm setting myself up for another case like Clay, all because I'm doing the radio show as opposed to the newspaper column. But you know what? I think he wouldn't be happy with even that." Diamond paused. "It doesn't matter. I have worked too hard and too long to let a few idiots stop me from doing what I love."

"Look, I wouldn't worry about it. Paul will think about it and realize that one weird call is no reason to get all bent out of shape. I'm sure he'll feel better about it today. And Paul knows how important your career is to you. He'll come around."

"I hope so."

The door chimes sang, and Tara looked up to see a man enter with a bouquet of white roses. Sharnette and her boyfriend must have had another fight.

"Definitely call me later. We'll do something if you can fit it in before you head to the station." Tara watched as Sharnette dealt with the deliveryman.

"All right, cuz. Thanks for listening."

After dealing with Sharnette, the deliveryman headed toward Tara's desk, surprising her. "Um, no problem, Diamond. You know I'm here for you. Uh, I've gotta go."

"Later."

The moment Tara hung up the phone, the deliveryman said to her, "Tara Montgomery?"

Tara eyed him warily. "Yes."

"These are for you."

Tara pushed back her chair and stood. "Me?" she asked, pointing a finger at herself. "How could they be for me?"

"Your name's on the bouquet," the man said with a smile. He placed the roses on her desk.

"Good Lord." It finally hit Tara that this huge arrangement of white roses and baby's breath was actually for her. "Is there a card?"

"It's in there."

"Wow."

The deliveryman turned, and Tara quickly said, "Wait." She dug into her purse for a tip, then passed it to him.

"Thanks, miss. Enjoy the flowers."

The man left, but no sooner was he gone, than Sharnette and Janice were at her side. Sarah, who was on the phone, watched them as she talked.

Tara was closest to Janice and Sharnette. They often hooked up after work for dinner or a drink.

"Well, don't just stand there," Sharnette said. "Open the card before I do it for you."

Tara quickly snatched the card from the bouquet, then held it protectively to her chest. *Harris,* she thought. *He's sending me the roses to let me know he's sorry for everything and that he wants me to forgive him.*

"I knew Harris would come around sooner or

later," Tara announced, opening the envelope's flap.

"If he wants to apologize," Janice began, "he should call—and call when he knows he's going to reach you and not your answering machine. Though the roses are beautiful." She bent her head and sniffed the bouquet.

Tara was nervous, and her fingers trembled as she pulled out the card. But her heart stopped when she saw the words scrawled on it.

"What is it?" Sharnette asked. She rounded the desk and stood beside Tara, then peered over her shoulder.

"It's not from Harris," she replied, her tone deadpan.

"Then who's it from?" Janice raised a curious eyebrow.

"Darren."

"Darren?" Sharnette asked, surprised. "I've never heard you talk about any Darren."

"The guy who was here yesterday," Tara explained matter-of-factly. "You remember him. The hottie."

A startled gasp escaped Sharnette's lips as a smile spread on her face. "Let me see that card."

Tara passed it to her.

"The beauty of these roses pales in comparison to your smile," Sharnette read. "Oh my, oh my. Tara! The man is serious."

"And he sounds romantic," Janice added. She reached for the card and Sharnette passed it to her.

Janice and Sharnette fussed over the card, but Tara tuned them out. She couldn't help the measure of disappointment she felt. More so, she felt like a fool. How for a moment she'd actually entertained the idea that Harris would send her roses was beyond her. Any man who could get engaged to someone else without even ending his relationship with her first had no scruples, much less the sense to ask for forgiveness. Even if he was sorry, Tara doubted Harris would ever be man enough to admit that.

"Tara."

Tara jerked her eyes from the floor to Sharnette's face. "Huh?"

"I said, are you going to call him? He left his number."

"Oh." Tara waved a hand, dismissing the idea. "I don't know about that."

Tara pushed back her chair. Sharnette and Janice stared at her. As Tara sank into her chair, Sharnette sat on the corner of the desk, while Janice stood beside her.

"If I were you, I'd call him," Janice said. "What do you have to lose?"

"And like I said before," Sharnette began, "you need a palette cleanser. Darren certainly fits the bill."

"I don't think so," Tara replied.

"It's exactly what you need," Sharnette countered. "Maybe then you'll stop walking around here with a frown."

Tara opened the file she was currently working on. "Sharnette, you are a trip."

"She's got a point," Janice chimed.

Tara gawked at her. "Enough! You two, I love you, but I am not going to talk about this anymore. I have work to do. Sharnette, did you get that ticket out by courier for Mrs. Hancock? She needs it by tomorrow."

"Sure, avoid the issue," Sharnette said.

"Did you?" Tara repeated sternly.

"Yes, of course." Sharnette linked arms with Janice. "Come on, Janice. Before she decides to can us."

Tara watched Sharnette and Janice walk away, giggling.

Then she rolled her eyes, and buried her face in the file.

"Tara, you have a call on line one," Sharnette announced hours later.

"Thanks." Tara hurried back to her desk, where she clicked the blinking extension. "Wholesale Travel, Tara speaking."

"Hello, Tara."

Tara's heart stopped. The greeting was casual, indicating it was someone she knew. And considering it wasn't Harris . . . "Hello?"

"Did you receive the roses?"

Oh, Lord. It *was* him. She cleared her throat, trying to regain her composure. "Yes. Yes, I did. Thank you. They're beautiful."

"I'm glad you like them."

Tara's eyes ventured to the corner of her desk, where the roses sat. The arrangement was definitely gorgeous. But it was too much. She barely knew Darren, and she felt uncomfortable about the gift. "Thanks again. But, Darren, please don't—"

"No strings attached," Darren said quickly. "Beautiful flowers for a beautiful lady, that's all." Pause. "However, I'm hoping you'll reconsider having dinner with me."

Tara sighed. "Darren, I'm flattered. I truly am. I

just . . . I don't think it's the best thing. Not at this point in my life, anyway. Like I told you before, it's not personal."

"All right."

Tara was slightly surprised that Darren didn't push the issue. "I'm glad you understand."

"But know that the offer still stands, should you ever change your mind."

"Thank you. Now, I really have to get back to work. I do have your number. . . ."

"Enjoy the rest of your day."

"You too. Good-bye."

Tara hung up, and was surprised at the feeling of frustration that swept over her. She'd expected to feel relieved.

She wanted to be angry with Darren, but he made it impossible. He was nice, and patient, and so darn understanding.

It bothered her to realize that at any other time, his attention would be flattering. Why did it irk her now?

She glanced in Sharnette's direction. Her colleague was on a call, thank the Lord. If she knew it had been Darren on the phone, she'd start up with that bit about using him as a palette cleanser again.

Tara inhaled deeply, remembering the sight of Darren's gorgeous body and beautiful smile. If she wanted a palette cleanser, he'd certainly fit the bill. . . .

What is wrong with you? she thought a second later. Shaking her head, she went back to work, though she couldn't erase the silly smirk that had made its way onto her face.

Six

Tara decided to leave work a couple of hours early that day. It had been slow anyway, and after talking with Diamond again, she realized how much they both needed a break. Besides her thinking about Darren every time she looked at the roses, Harris had crept into her mind. She supposed it was only natural, but it was high time she got back into gear and tried to get over the man.

She and Diamond had decided on a late afternoon movie, which would give Diamond plenty of time to get to work to prepare for her late-night talk show. They'd decided on something funny. Neither of them wanted any romance on the brain tonight.

Tara climbed behind the wheel of her Ford Focus and left downtown Miami. She was thankful to beat the rush-hour traffic.

She called her mother on her way home, just to assure her that she was okay. Her mother lived in Miramar, as did her aunt and uncle—Diamond's parents. Everyone was worried about her since her breakup with Harris. She'd kept a somewhat low profile from her family, because she couldn't deal with their empathy.

The only positive side of all this was that her father wasn't alive to know of Harris's betrayal. He'd always loved Harris, and had considered him a son.

Tara felt a moment of sadness as she thought of her father. He'd passed just over two years ago, but she still missed him dearly. She supposed she always would.

When Tara reached her neighborhood, she pulled into the Winn Dixie Plaza. She hadn't been eating much since the fiasco with Harris, and her fridge was embarrassingly bare. If Diamond decided to stop by before the movie or afterward, she needed to have something to give her!

She parked her car, and minutes later, was inside the store. She knew what she wanted—rather, needed. Just the essentials. Milk, bread, juice, eggs. It didn't take her more than five minutes to gather all the items she wanted and pay for them.

"See you later, Arlene," Tara told the cashier as she left. She'd been coming to this store for the past five years that she'd lived in this neighborhood and knew practically all the staff.

"Take care," Arlene replied, the slight Hispanic accent sounding in her words.

Tara headed toward the doors and stepped outside. Instantly, she frowned. In the few minutes she'd been inside, the sky had turned dark gray. It was drizzling.

Tara continued walking, but halted when she heard the loud roar of thunder. Just like that, the rain came down in heavy sheets.

Just what I need, she thought, grimacing. In an instant, the weather had gone from sun to rain—an everyday occurrence during the summer in Florida.

The problem was, she'd left her umbrella in the

car. It wasn't far, but she'd surely get soaked as she ran across the grocery store parking lot with her bags of groceries.

"Looks like you need this."

Tara whirled at the sound of the now-familiar voice. Behind her stood Darren Burkeen.

He flashed her a sweet smile.

Tara blinked, momentarily unable to believe that it was really him. Since when did he live in this neighborhood?

But the question left her mind as she looked at the proffered umbrella. In weather like this, it was a godsend.

"I—" Tara stopped. Sure, Darren was definitely a nice guy, but she had no intentions of leading him on. "No, thank you. A few raindrops never killed anyone."

"Then at least let me help you with your bags."

Before Tara could say a word, he reached for the few bags she held, taking them from her.

The guy didn't miss a beat.

Her groceries in one hand, Darren popped open the umbrella with his other. The protest that had been forming on Tara's lips died.

The man is only offering to carry your groceries and keep you dry. What's the harm in that?

Darren turned and looked at her, his expression saying that he was waiting for her to join him beneath the umbrella. Taking a step toward him, Tara offered him a small smile.

"You don't have any bags," she commented as they started for the parking lot. Rain splashed at her legs as they left the protective cover of the grocery store awning. "Did I take you away from your shopping?"

"I was heading inside to pick something up when I saw you standing outside the store. Which way's your car?"

"To the left," she replied. "Near the back. I'm never one of those lucky people who pulls up just as someone is driving out of a spot at the front."

Darren chuckled softly. "I hear you. I'm usually not that lucky either. But hey, maybe our luck's going to change."

At his words, Tara's eyes lifted to his. Her pulse quickened. There was no mistaking it; he was referring to the two of them, to what the future might hold in terms of a relationship.

She looked away. "Darren, I really think you're a nice man. And for that reason, I don't want to lead you on."

"Uh-oh." But there was a smile in his voice.

Tara's throat went dry, her words dying. How could she say anything that might hurt him when he was being so . . . so sweet? She cleared her throat and went on. "It's not you, Darren. It's . . . it's me," she finished lamely, knowing how clichéd that was. "Under any other circumstances, I wouldn't mind getting to know you. But I've just come out of a five-year relationship, and I'm really not ready."

"You were involved with Harris Seeman?"

Tara abruptly stopped. "How—how did you know?"

"Someone in your office. When I called today, she told me what had happened before she transferred my call to you."

Sharnette. Tara hadn't known that Sharnette had realized Darren was on the line. But considering Sharnette had given Darren personal information about her, it was no wonder she hadn't quickly come over to get the scoop from her about the call. She'd probably expected Tara to approach her after she'd learned what she had said.

Tara could easily imagine Sharnette blurting out her personal business, in a misguided attempt to help her out.

Brother! She wondered when Sharnette and Janice would cut her some slack about the lack of her love life.

Maybe once she cleansed her palette . . .

Embarrassed at the direction of her thoughts, Tara quickly said, "Okay, so you know about Harris and how he recently hurt me. Then you understand my position?"

"Yes, I understand—I understand that he was a fool. I don't know how any man in his right frame of mind could do that to you, of all people."

Such a sweet thing for him to say, but he really didn't know her.

"I suppose he thought he had his reasons."

"He was a coward. You deserve much better." Darren's eyes met and held hers for a long moment. Then he began to walk again. "Which one's your car?"

Such a short look, but it had sent a charge through her entire body. "Um, the red one. Fourth car up on the right."

Once they were there, Tara opened the door and Darren placed her grocery bags on the passenger's seat. And even though the rain had started to let up, he sheltered her with the umbrella as she went to the driver's side and got in.

"By the way." Darren held the car door a moment before closing it.

Inwardly, Tara cringed. Here it came. The offer to take her to dinner or a movie.

"In case you're wondering," he went on, "I'm not a stalker." He softened the serious words with a grin. "I actually live in the area. I don't know how I missed you before, but I'm certainly glad I got the chance to make your acquaintance. Have a good evening."

Then he closed the door, leaving Tara feeling a measure of confusion as he turned and headed back toward the grocery store.

Seven

"Why don't you just call him?" Diamond suggested.

Tara stopped dead in her tracks and faced her cousin. The two were leaving Sunset Plaza where they'd spent the afternoon shopping, followed up with an early evening movie. A comedy again, like they'd seen a few days earlier. It was a girls' day out, where they could shoot the breeze about what was going on in their lives.

But Diamond's comment completely caught Tara off guard. "Excuse me?" she asked.

"You realize that every free moment you've had from the time I met you to see this movie, you've talked about Darren? You did the same thing a few days ago when I saw you, too."

"Because I can't believe him," Tara replied quickly. "He sent me flowers again yesterday."

"Yes, I know."

"And I'm still thinking about how I ran into him at Winn Dixie—"

"Sounds like you're thinking about him, period."

"Let me finish," Tara said. "I've never seen the guy in my neighborhood before; then suddenly he's there when I'm coming out of the grocery store? Was that really a coincidence?"

"Oh, so now he's a stalker?" Diamond chuckled.

Tara gave her cousin a pointed look. "You of all people shouldn't make light of such a situation, Diamond."

"And I wouldn't—if that's what I thought it was. But I know you, Tara. And I haven't heard you talk nonstop about someone since—since you met Harris."

"That's not—" But unsure of her own words, Tara quickly continued up the stairs to the parking garage.

"Obviously you're attracted to him. And everyone knows the best way to get over one guy is to get involved with another."

Rolling her eyes, Tara opened the door to the parking garage.

"And quit rolling your eyes. You know it's true."

Tara couldn't help smiling. Her cousin knew her so well. Holding the door open, Tara turned to her. "You sound just like Sharnette."

"Hey, I've always said that Sharnette is good people."

Tara scowled at her as she walked past her into the garage.

"I don't see why you don't want to get to know Darren . . . a little better." She chuckled. "I think it might do you a world of good."

Tara guffawed. "Jumping right into a relationship with someone else is definitely trouble."

"This is the twenty-first century. Go with the flow. Besides, calling the man doesn't mean you're committing to anything other than getting to know him. Get your mind out of the gutter!"

"Oh, you're too funny."

"Seriously, cuz. What's it going to hurt to spend some time with him?"

"Enough already!" Tara exclaimed as she reached her car. "Notice how you're deliberately avoiding talking about Paul?"

"There's nothing to say. Ever since he apologized a couple days ago, he's been cool. And I haven't seen him much, anyway. You know, our schedules."

Tara got into her Focus, and Diamond got in beside her. "You could be spending the day with him, since this is a day off for both of you."

"I could be. But I'm here with you."

Despite Diamond's nonchalant attitude, Tara could sense that Diamond's relationship with Paul was still on rocky ground, and that was why she wasn't spending time with him right now.

"So, no more weird calls?" Tara began to back out of the spot.

"No, nothing. I'm even more convinced now that it was a weird prank."

Tara wasn't completely convinced, but she wasn't sure they should be overly concerned until there was a reason to be. "I'm sure you're right."

"So when do I get to meet this Darren guy?" Diamond asked, bringing the subject back to Tara.

"Shut up!" Tara exclaimed. But she was laughing.

The following Monday morning, when a delivery-man arrived at Tara's office with an impressive balloon arrangement, complete with teddy bear, Tara's heart stopped.

It was just after noon, and Sharnette had gone

for her lunch break. Sarah sat at the receptionist's desk.

Janice, whose desk was to the front and left of Tara's desk, shot Tara a quick glance as the deliveryman stopped in front of Sarah.

Please don't let it be—

"Yes, Tara is right there," Sarah announced, pointing in her direction.

The deliveryman approached her, smiling. "Someone's either trying to apologize, or he's trying to get to know you."

"I don't believe it," Tara said softly.

"Here you go." The man placed the teddy bear and balloons on her desk. It was then that Tara noticed the box of chocolates.

"Thank you so much," she said. She took some money from her purse and tipped the man.

No sooner was he out the door than Janice practically sprinted to her desk.

"I swear, people are soon going to start confusing Wholesale Travel for Wholesale Flowers and Gifts."

"God . . . I don't know what to say." *Much less think.*

The doorbells chimed, and Tara looked up to see that Sharnette had returned. Her face instantly exploded in an ear-to-ear grin.

"Ooooh." Sharnette hurried to Tara's desk. "I leave the office for a few minutes and I miss the day's excitement?"

"Look at this arrangement." Janice fingered the box of chocolates. "Godiva. The man has taste."

"I can't believe he's doing this."

"You must have left some kind of impression on him, that much is obvious."

Tara looked up at Janice. "That's the thing. After

running into him at Winn Dixie, I figured he'd finally understood. Then he sends me more flowers on Friday. Now this?"

It didn't get better for the rest of the week.

More flowers on Tuesday. Chocolates on Wednesday. A gigantic stuffed monkey on Thursday. Tara barely fit it in her trunk.

On Friday, Tara went to the door when she saw the deliveryman approaching through the glass. She recognized him, even though his face wasn't obscured by a huge bouquet today.

"Hello, Tara."

"Hey, Jeff."

Jeff passed her the single red rose, and the accompanying card. As Tara accepted the items, he said, "Don't you think it's time you called the man?"

Tara only grinned.

"There's something to be said for a man who's persistent," Sharnette commented when Jeff had gone.

A single red rose. In so many ways, this gift was the most poignant.

Tara brought the rose to her nose and inhaled the sweet scent as she stood in front of Sharnette's desk, a smile creeping onto her face as she did.

She removed the card and read: "A good thing is worth waiting for. I hope this brightens your day."

"Girl, he's got it bad," Sharnette said.

Janice appeared beside her. "Did he leave his number again?"

"Yes." Tara smiled. He had to know she already had it.

"Well, are you going to put it to use finally?"

"I suppose if I don't, we *will* soon have to change

the name of the business to Wholesale Floral Shop."
She held the rose to her lips.

"I'm kinda interested in seeing how far this man
will take this," Janice commented.

"Me too."

"Well, you're not going to find out. I will call the
man and put him out of his misery."

Truth be told, Tara was also curious to know how
long Darren would continue sending her flowers,
chocolates, and gifts if she simply didn't call him.

But she'd only be punishing herself if she didn't
call him.

Because she was definitely looking forward to seeing him.

Ever since reaching his answering service, Tara
had been waiting to hear back from Darren. As
much as she tried to deny it, she'd felt a tingling of
disappointment in her stomach when she hadn't
reached him personally, and she couldn't help wondering if he was going to get back to her.

Whenever the phone rang, she got her hopes
up . . . only to be disappointed.

But just after three, when the phone rang again,
Sharnette announced, "Tara, this call's for you. I
think it's *him.*"

Tara swallowed while Sharnette transferred the
call. She opted for the receiver as opposed to her
headset, and casually said, "Hello?"

"Hello, Tara," came the reply.

There was no mistaking that deep, sexy voice. A
smile spread on Tara's face. "Hey, there."

"I got your message."

"Yes. Yes, I called." Nervous, Tara looked across

the office. Both Sharnette and Janice stared at her
with wide eyes. Tara quickly dropped her gaze to
her desk. "Finally."

"I was wondering if you were going to."

"Well, you wore me down. And I mean that in
the best possible way." She paused. "You truly are
spoiling me."

"Something tells me you deserve a little spoiling."

In all the time she had been with Harris, he
hadn't romanced her the way Darren had. It was
something she could get used to. How could any
normal woman not?

Tara exhaled a shaky breath. "I've been thinking . . . and if your offer for dinner still stands—"

"Are you free tonight?" came the question.

But his tone was light, and both Darren and Tara
laughed.

"Actually, if you're serious . . . yeah. I can spare
some time tonight."

"I will make time. How's seven?"

"That'll work."

"Shall I pick you up? Or do you want to meet me
somewhere?"

"Hmm." Tara thought about his suggestion. To
be on the safe side, she'd be better off meeting him
somewhere. If the date went horribly, she could always leave early in her own car and not worry about
any hassles. "Let's meet."

"Anyplace special?" Darren asked.

"I don't know." Glancing at Sharnette, Tara saw
that she was pretending to work. What the hell. Let
her listen. Sharnette and Janice would grill her for
all the details of the call later, anyway. "I like The

Cheesecake Factory. And On The Border is a great spot, too."

"I've never been to On The Border," Darren commented. "The one by Kendall Drive and the turnpike?"

"Yes, that's the one."

"Then let's meet there."

"Seven o'clock," Tara said, confirming the time. "See you then."

Replacing the receiver, Tara sighed happily. "I'm meeting him," she announced, though she knew her colleagues had already heard her. "For dinner."

"Oooh." Sharnette's nose wrinkled as she flashed a hundred-watt smile. "Bye-bye, Harris. Hello, Palette Cleanser."

"Whatever!" Tara swirled around in her swivel chair, then settled her elbows on the desk. Darren was most definitely not the kind of guy one used simply as a palette cleanser.

She could hardly wait to see him.

Right on time, Tara saw Darren exit a black Nissan Pathfinder and start toward the restaurant door. He saw her almost instantly, and despite the several feet between them and the fact that the sky was darkening, Tara could see the warmth that filled his eyes.

Tara's heart jolted at the look. Goodness, it had been so long, she'd forgotten that special thrill that came when first getting to know someone you were attracted to. Already, she was glad she'd agreed to spend some time with Darren.

She certainly didn't know where this might lead, but she was also very aware that it was too soon to be thinking of anything more than one day at a time. Dating someone nice would be a great way to take her mind off Harris, and to get back into the flow of being single.

As Darren stepped toward the door, Tara stepped forward and opened it for him. He beamed down at her, those gorgeous dimples winking at her.

"Hi," Tara said.

"Hi." Darren wrapped his arms around her, enveloping her in an eager hug.

The hug made Tara feel warm all over.

When Darren pulled apart from her, he said, "Ready to head inside?"

"Yep. There's a bit of a waiting list, but we're already on it."

They took a seat on the wooden bench in the restaurant's lobby. Tara took her time settling, drawing her purse onto her lap. She wasn't quite sure what to say all of a sudden—and she certainly didn't want to say anything stupid.

With nothing left to fiddle with, Tara finally turned to Darren. Once again, she felt a zap hit her body. There was something special about him that you could sense just from looking into his eyes.

"So." Tara gave him a smile. "In all this time you've been sending me flowers and cards and candies, I don't believe you ever told me what you do."

"For a living, you mean?"

"Yes."

"I'm an insurance adjuster for Westgate Insurance."

"Really?"

"Mmm-hmm. Have been for twelve years."

"What exactly does an insurance adjuster do?"

"For one, I'm what's known as a road adjuster. I

work on the road, heading out to take care of personal and commercial property claims, such as water damage to a house, a ceiling caving in, wind damage, et cetera. Once, I went out to assess a claim for an explosion due to hydroponics."

"You're kidding."

"Nope. Someone was growing pot in a back room of their house, and they must've done something wrong, because there was an explosion, resulting in damage to the house."

"I can't believe someone would call you because of that!"

"Truth is stranger than fiction, believe me." Darren paused. "It's basically the adjuster's job to get to the bottom of things . . . and not give too much in terms of money to the insured. I know, I know. People tend to dislike adjusters. We control the money flow from the insurance company. Most often, the public perception is that we don't give enough money to cover things, but that's because no one really reads the insurance company's policy."

"Oh, is that so?"

"It's the truth. Anyway, as you can imagine, this results in a lot of arguments between the adjuster and the insured. This happens a lot."

"So you head out to scenes of trauma and disaster, people get on your case because they don't think you give them enough money, yet you seem like a man who doesn't carry any burdens on his shoulders."

"Life is too short to spend it being miserable."

"So you like your job?"

Darren half nodded, half shrugged. "Yeah. It's a job. I don't work nine to five, which is nice in a lot

of ways. But then I can be called out in the middle
of the night to the scene of a fatal accident."

"If you put as much effort into your job as you
did in wooing me"—Tara smiled—"I imagine
you're good at it. I imagine you're good at anything
you do."

Darren's eyes met and held hers, and he reached
for one of her hands. "I try my best."

The words "I want you" were written all over his
face. Tara inhaled a deep breath, but her heart still
pounded at the meaning behind his words. She was
enjoying this feeling she'd long forgotten.

Still, she was shy. She hadn't dealt with a man as
forthright and charming as Darren before. She had
no clue what she was supposed to do, to say.

She lowered her head. Darren placed a finger beneath her chin, and she lifted her gaze to his. He
just stared at her, but didn't say a word.

It seemed as if time stood still.

"You really do have the most beautiful eyes," Darren said after a long while. "They mesmerize me."

"Montgomery, party of two," came the announcement from the hostess stand.

"That's us," Tara announced, standing.

The young hostess escorted them to a small
booth.

When they sat, Tara began, "I told the hostess
nonsmoking because I didn't know if you smoked
or not. I hope that was okay."

"Definitely. I don't smoke."

"Good." That was a relief. Tara didn't like the
smell of cigarette smoke, much less the taste of it.
Here she was, considering the idea of kissing Darren. . . . "Neither do I."

Darren raised an eyebrow as he looked at her. "Anything else you want to know about me?"

Tara shrugged. "Everything, I guess."

"Okay. I was born in Jamaica, but emigrated when I was twelve. Believe it or not, my family went to Minneapolis."

"Minneapolis? That had to be a culture shock."

"Tell me about it. I had an aunt who was living there, so we moved there and she helped us get our start in this country. But I'm an island boy at heart, so you don't have to wonder why I relocated to South Florida the moment I had a chance."

Tara chuckled. "I guess not."

"I came down here for spring break my senior year of high school, and that's when it clicked that there was another place I could live in the U.S. and be happy. I didn't have to suffer through winter, waiting for warmth and sunshine. I knew I had to head back here as soon as possible."

"And what about the rest of your family?"

"They're still in Minneapolis."

"Brothers and sisters?"

A flicker of pain clouded his face. "I had a sister."

"Oh, no. Had?"

"Yes." Darren nodded grimly. "Tracy. She was a year younger than I, and she . . . she died. She was seventeen."

Tara extended her hand across the table and covered his hands with hers. "I'm so sorry." When Darren didn't say another word, Tara asked, "Want to tell me about it?"

"Not really."

She shouldn't take it personally, but she felt a tinge of sadness at the fact that he was closing her off. But she understood.

"I lost my father a little over two years ago, and I know how hard it is to lose someone close to you."

"It was *very* hard. Almost impossible to deal with." Darren exhaled loudly, and the sad sound made Tara's heart ache. "My trip to Florida was a couple months after her death. It was something my parents had encouraged me to do, and my friends, because I'd been depressed after losing Tracy."

Tara shook her head sadly.

"Weather aside, the bigger part of my reason for moving to Florida was that I needed a new scene after losing my sister. A fresh start, where not every place reminded me of her."

"I understand." She squeezed his hands.

Darren sat back, resting his hands on his lap. "Well, that was a long time ago."

"But you never truly get over it."

Darren shrugged. "I guess not."

"Any regrets?"

"About moving to Florida?"

"Mmm-hmm."

Darren's eyes locked on hers. He leaned forward and reached for her hand once again. "None."

Eight

Before they even finished their dinner, Tara found herself wishing time would slow down. She didn't want her time with Darren to end.

He was fun. All through their evening, he'd entertained her with stories of what it was like working as an insurance adjuster, and the types of scams people tried to pull.

She was grateful for the easy way he led a conversation. The easy way he made her laugh and smile.

Time flew too quickly. As Tara pushed her plate away and sat back, the waitress appeared. "Let me take those plates for you," she said. Then, "Can I interest either of you in dessert?"

Both Tara and Darren said in unison, "No."

Tara giggled. "I'm stuffed."

"Me too," Darren said.

"Okay, here's the bill." Balancing the plates with one arm, the waitress dug the bill out of her apron with her free hand. She placed it on the table before Darren. "Thanks, guys. Have a great night."

Darren looked at the bill, then reached into his wallet and took out money.

"You ready?" he asked Tara.

"Sure."

They both slipped out of the booth and stood. As they headed for the door, Darren placed a gentle hand on her back. Tara couldn't help feeling a moment of regret. She'd truly enjoyed the time she'd spent with Darren, and the night had ended too soon.

Outside, Darren stopped and faced her. "I know you only planned on dinner," he began, "but if you don't have anything else to do right now—"

"I'd love to," Tara quickly replied.

He gazed down at her, pleasant surprise in his eyes.

Tara grinned at him. "What did you have in mind?"

"It's Friday night. There are endless things to do. We can find a place to go dancing, or maybe take a walk at Bayside."

"You know, I work so close to Bayside, but I hardly get there." The Bayside Marketplace was arguably Miami's most popular tourist attraction. Situated along the shores of Biscayne Bay, it housed over a hundred shops, and offered dining and entertainment, as well as a number of boat tours.

"I was thinking Bayside. A nice place to walk and get to know each other, perhaps have a nightcap."

"That sounds nice."

"You want to take my car? I don't see the sense in taking two. Since we both live in this area, I can drop you off back here and you'll be close to home."

"Sure," Tara agreed. She trusted Darren, and she wanted to spend as much time getting to know him as possible. "Lead the way."

Darren gave her a smile, then took her hand in his and led her to the parking lot.

The lively sounds of salsa filled the air as Tara and Darren walked toward Bayside. Once through one of the arches that led to the open-air complex, they could see the salsa band performing on the marina stage that bordered the bay, crowded by happy spectators. Palm trees laced with tiny lights sparkled in the darkness of the night. A yacht with several people on deck sailed in the bay, its lights glistening on the water's gentle ripples.

"This is so beautiful," Tara commented. "I can't believe I hardly come here."

"People always forget about what's in their own backyards. Which is a shame in a place like Miami. There's so much to do here."

A crowd of laughing women rushed by Tara and Darren. One of the women bumped into Tara, causing her to stumble against Darren. Instantly, he secured his arms around her.

Regaining her balance in his strong arms, she looked up at him. Instinctively, Tara knew that Darren was the kind of man who wouldn't think before protecting her, and that reality made her feel warm right down to her toes.

"Easy now," he said.

"Thanks."

Even though he could have, he didn't release her. Instead, he kept his arm draped around her waist as they started walking once more.

"Where to?" Darren asked.

"Let's walk."

Darren strolled with her toward the water. The

sounds of the music serenaded them, and though there were people all around, Tara felt as if they were the only two people there.

She looked out at the marina, at the various private boats docked along the quay wall. One of the tour boats was several feet to the right. People came to Bayside all the time to take dinner cruises. She remembered having suggested this to Harris, and while he'd promised to take her on such a cruise, he'd never gotten around to it.

"What are you thinking?" Darren asked.

Tara hesitated.

"Honestly," Darren added.

"Don't take this the wrong way," Tara began. "But I was thinking about . . . about Harris. How he'd always promised to take me on a dinner cruise and never did."

"That's a shame."

"When I think about it, there were so many things he said we'd do, but we hardly did any of them."

"He didn't take you out? Wine you and dine you?"

"We went for dinner at least once every month."

Darren abruptly stopped his casual stroll and faced her. "Once a month?"

Tara thought a moment. "Yeah."

"Now that's definitely a shame. A man has a beautiful woman like you and he doesn't take her out?"

"I don't think that it's because he didn't want to, but because . . . well, because he had a goal. For his career. He worked a lot of hours, and I guess . . . I guess it paid off." The image of his photo with the boss's daughter announcing their engagement flooded her mind. She cringed.

"Seems he lost what should have been most important to him."

Tara merely shrugged. Stepping away from Darren, she walked to the marina's edge and glanced down at the water.

Seconds later, she sensed his presence behind her. "You were involved with him a long time. You're not going to forget him overnight."

Tara turned then. Darren wore a gentle, understanding expression. "I know you're right," she said. "It's just that I'm with you, and I don't want to be thinking about him at all."

"Are you still in love with him?"

"No. My love for him died the day I learned that he'd betrayed me so heartlessly." Tara paused. "But it's weird . . . I still think about him. I guess in a lot of ways, I miss him. Sorry. This isn't what you want to hear."

Darren didn't respond. Moving beside her, he stared out at the water as well.

"What about you?" Tara asked. "Did any woman ever break your heart?"

"Yeah."

A beat. "You want to tell me about it?"

"It ended three years ago. I loved her, but she wasn't the woman I thought she was. She was a Jamaican citizen, and unfortunately, only interested in finding a man who would marry her so she could stay in this country."

Tara faced him, but he still looked out at the water. She studied his profile. "I'm sorry."

"It's not your fault."

"Do you miss her?"

"I think about her from time to time. I guess I wonder what it would have been like, if she'd been sincere." Darren faced her. "But then I realize how pointless it is to think like that. She *wasn't* the person she claimed to be, so everything was a lie. It makes no sense to wonder what would have been when your hopes and dreams were based on a lie."

It was strange, but hearing of Darren's lost love made Tara feel a little better. Like she wasn't the only person in the world who'd suffered a broken heart. Logically, she knew she wasn't, but hearing of someone else's heartache reminded her that she wasn't alone.

And that she would move on.

Tara ran her hand down Darren's arm. "Seems like we've both been involved with our share of fools."

Darren smiled.

There was a round of applause, and Darren looked beyond Tara's shoulder. The band had finished their song. Moments later, they started up with another lively salsa tune.

"Feel like dancing?" Darren asked.

"Me?" Tara pointed to herself. "Uh, no. I'm not a dancer."

"Oh, come on. . . ." Darren slipped his arms around her waist.

"No!" Tara protested, giggling as she moved away from him. "You'd only be disappointed."

"I doubt anything you do would disappoint me."

His words sent a ripple of desire pulsing through her. She swallowed. "I assure you, you don't want to see me dance."

"You grew up in South Florida, didn't you?"

"Yes, and I've learned only a few words in Spanish, and I certainly didn't learn to salsa or tango or—" Tara stopped abruptly when Darren placed a palm over her cheek. "Why—why are you looking at me like—"

"You don't believe me, do you?"

"About what?"

"About your eyes. That they're the most mesmerizing I've ever seen."

Uncomfortable, Tara glanced away. "I believe . . . I believe that you are very charming."

"Meaning I know exactly the right thing to say, truth or not?"

"Well, kind of."

"Ouch. That hurt." Darren's lips went downward in a mock-hurt expression.

Tara laughed. "You're silly."

Darren pulled her close, surprising her. "And you need to believe me." He paused, staring deeply into her eyes for several seconds. "I don't lie to get what I want. But I do speak the truth, directly."

Tara's breath snagged in her throat. "I do believe that."

"And right now, in case there's any misunderstanding, I want you to know that I'm attracted to you."

"Are you?"

Darren brushed his nose across her cheek. "Very."

Butterflies went wild in Tara's stomach. She closed her eyes and savored the feeling of being in his arms. She could definitely get used to this.

"I want to kiss you," he whispered into her ear. "Can I?"

Nervous laughter escaped Tara's throat. Most men didn't ask if they could kiss a woman. "You really are something else."

"In a good way, I hope." He pulled back and looked into her eyes.

"Yes. Most definitely."

And then his face was moving toward hers, as if in slow motion. Tara was aware of all the sensations flooding her body—desire, anticipation, fear, and that sweet nervousness that came the very first time you were going to kiss someone.

His mouth skimmed hers once, twice. Then his lips were on her cheek, her chin, and finally back at her mouth.

Tara sighed, her lips parting. Darren's mouth moved softly over hers, suckling, nibbling. And when he framed her face with both hands, the pace of the kiss went from slow and easy to fire and need. He delved his tongue into her mouth, flicking it over hers. Tara's mouth opened wider, taking all that Darren had to offer. Heat washed over her, making her dizzy.

With a soft moan of pleasure, Darren ended the kiss, resting his lips on her forehead.

"Wow."

Darren pulled back and grinned at her.

"Oh, God. Did I just say that?" Tara hadn't meant to speak aloud.

"Yes, and I'll take that as a compliment."

A smile played on Tara's lips. Then suddenly, she yawned.

"Hmm. I guess I should take that as my cue."

"I am a little tired," Tara confessed. "It's been an interesting week at work. I haven't slept much."

"Then let me get you back to your car."

"No, we don't have to go. Didn't you want a nightcap?"

Darren linked his hand with Tara's. "We can do that another time."

"Are you sure?" Tara yawned again.

"Yes, I'm sure."

Darren started off, but Tara pulled on his hand, stopping him. Darren turned to face her.

A soft smile touched her lips. "I just wanted to say . . . I had a really great time tonight, Darren."

"I had a great time, too."

"And . . . I'd like to do it again sometime, if you would."

"Absolutely," he replied, and winked.

Tara may have been tired when she left Darren, but when she got home, she was too wired to sleep. All she could think about was Darren and the incredible evening she'd spent with him.

Her mind replayed the entire date, over and over. Every time she closed her eyes and tried to sleep, she remembered the thrill she'd felt when Darren had held her hand in his, when he'd wrapped his arms around her, and how warm and wonderful she'd felt inside when he'd kissed her.

If Diamond wasn't at work, Tara would have called her, because she needed someone to talk to about her evening. As much as she wouldn't have imagined it, she was attracted to Darren more than she had ever anticipated.

Everything she knew about him was positive. There was nothing that she didn't like. Nothing most women wouldn't like.

Compared to Harris . . . Well, there really was no comparison. Darren was completely romantic; for him, being so came with ease. Harris had done some romantic things in his life, but doing so certainly wasn't part of his nature.

In fact, Tara had often reminded Harris of the special occasions in their lives—like her birthday. Even Valentine's Day. If she didn't ask if he had something planned for them ahead of time, he normally forgot.

Tara hadn't minded—totally. In the beginning she had, but then she'd gotten used to it. She had told herself that it didn't matter that Harris didn't surprise her for special occasions, because love was a 365-day-a-year commitment. Consistency was key, what mattered most.

But after one night with Darren, she now knew what she'd been missing out on.

A lot.

Sighing happily, Tara rolled from her back onto her side. No matter what she did, she couldn't put Darren out of her mind.

She reached for the radio and turned it on. Diamond's smooth voice filled the airwaves instantly.

"C'mon, sister. You know you were wrong. I don't care how cute the man is, or how great he is in bed, dating your sister's ex is one of the basic no-nos!"

"But, Lady D, if I could tell you all the things my sister has done to me—"

"So is that why you're calling? So I can tell you that two wrongs make a right? You know I'm not going to tell you that. Just because your sister has hurt you, that's no reason to stoop to this level to hurt her. And you know I'm speaking the truth, or you wouldn't have called. Your conscience is eating at you. And the worst thing is, when this guy moves on, who's going to be hurt? You. So, it's not just your sister. You both lose in the end, and it sounds like this guy wins."

"You're probably right, Lady D."

"I know I am. Listen, I can hear in your voice that you want to patch things up with your sister. I wish you luck doing so."

"Thanks, Lady D."

"All right, my sister. You take care." Pause. "Sibling rivalry. It's a big issue, isn't it? And at the root of it all, everyone's afraid, insecure, whatever. Please, please, please, everyone. Sibling relationships are hard enough. Don't do anything to make them worse. Trust me, you will live to regret it.

"Broken hearts, sibling rivalries, taking a chance on someone new. Those are a few of the issues we've discussed so far tonight. Let's keep those hot topics coming. This is your time tonight, as it is every Monday to Friday night, from ten-thirty to midnight, right here on 93.1 on your FM dial. This is Lady D, and I'm your host for *The Love Chronicles* on Talk 93, South Florida's hottest talk radio. You can reach me at 555-2100 in Dade County, 555-7455 in Broward, and 555-3860 in Palm Beach County. Call me with whatever's on your mind. But first, we've got to pay some bills."

Taking a chance on someone new. Tara knew exactly what her cousin would tell her if she were a caller on Diamond's show, discussing the new man in her life. She'd tell her to forget about the old and ring in the new with grand style.

A smile playing on her lips, Tara shut the radio off and lay back.

Her cousin would be right. It would do her no good to let the pain of her past relationship keep her from opening her heart to finding someone new.

And Darren was a special man. There was no doubt about that.

Tara was tempted to call the radio station and leave a message for Diamond to call her back, no matter how late. She was so anxious to tell her how well her evening had gone.

Instead, Tara turned off the bedside lamp and snuggled under her sheets.

Tomorrow would come soon enough. She could fill her cousin in on all that had happened on her date then.

Now, she closed her eyes, and knew she'd dream of Darren.

Nine

"It was so . . . so . . . amazing," Tara finished. "Everything. I mean, the man is so romantic. And he has this way of never crossing the line to disrespect that leaves you wanting more. Most other guys, after a night like that, would be trying to take you home. Darren didn't even suggest it."

"He's a man who knows that good things are worth waiting for."

"I think he wrote that to me in one of the many cards he sent me." Tara hugged one of the sofa's pillows against her chest. Diamond sat on the other end of the sofa, her legs curled beneath her. "It's just so . . . old-fashioned."

"You're not complaining, are you? I wish some man with old-fashioned values would come and sweep me off my feet. The man understands the meaning of the word *chivalry*. I wish there were more like him around."

"Tell me about it."

Diamond's mouth curled in a smug look. "Was I right, or was I right?"

"Yes, you were right. I'm glad I went out with him."

"When's the next date?"

"I don't know. He's gonna call me. Maybe we'll do dinner and a movie midweek. Though I'm not sure I can wait that long."

"Then call him. This is the twenty-first century. He's been direct, telling you that he likes you. There's nothing wrong with you calling to ask him out on the second date." Diamond paused. "Sunday's a great day for dinner and a movie."

"Tomorrow?"

"Why not?"

Tara blew out a nervous breath. "I don't know, Diamond. Yes, I know that I like him, but in a way, it seems like things are moving so fast."

"But they're not. It's not like you've jumped into bed with him. You're getting to know him; there's nothing wrong with that. If you like the guy, why *not* spend as much time with him as you can? That's the best way to figure out if he's suitable for anything long term."

"Tomorrow?" Tara asked.

"Why not?"

"I think . . . I think I'll wait and see if he calls me first. If not, then I'll call him." Tara's stomach was already a ball of nerves at the mere suggestion. She dropped her head back against the sofa's headrest, then popped it back up. "I didn't even ask—any more strange calls at the station?"

"Nope."

It had been over two weeks since the first bizarre call. "That's good to hear."

"Yeah. I'm pretty sure it was just . . . just a prank. Someone being an idiot."

"No doubt."

"And the dreams I was having about Clay—

they've stopped. I guess I was more worried about the call than I cared to admit."

Tara did rest her head back then, the memory of Darren kissing her flashing into her mind.

"Girl, don't go off into la-la land. You can do that when I'm gone."

Lifting her head, Tara smiled. "I'm sorry."

Diamond waved a hand. "Oh, that's okay. You know I'm just bugging. But while you're up in the clouds, I'll share my good news with you."

"What?"

"The station is giving me another time slot."

"You're kidding?"

"Nope." Diamond's smile lit up her gorgeous eyes. "Starting in a week, I will have a late afternoon show as well."

"That's wonderful, Diamond!"

"My ratings keep getting better and better, and the station is so pleased. They're certain I can woo an afternoon audience."

"It's a blessing."

"It absolutely is. I thank God for everything good that's happening in my life."

Tara eyed her cousin warily. "But . . . ?"

"But." Diamond sighed. "But I haven't told Paul yet."

"Why not? You don't think he'll be happy for you?"

"I have a feeling he won't."

"Well, you can't keep this from him."

Diamond blew out a weary breath. "I know. The very fact that I'm dreading telling him says a lot. I think I've been avoiding some truths about our relationship."

"Diamond, you're not saying what I think you're saying. . . ."

She shrugged. "Maybe. I guess it depends on how he reacts to my news."

"I hope he supports you." Since her relationship with Tyrone had ended shortly after the nightmare with Clay, Diamond hadn't had a relationship that lasted longer than three months. At the first sign of trouble, Diamond ended things. Tara didn't want to see her cousin go through a string of broken relationships, all in the name of protecting her heart.

"I hope so too. Because if he doesn't, then it'll be obvious that he's not the man for me."

"Don't rush to judgment," Tara cautioned. "Maybe all you'll need to do is find a way to compromise. Come to an understanding. You've invested time and emotion into this new relationship. It'd be a shame to end it when things get a little tough."

Diamond shrugged nonchalantly, as though the idea of ending yet another relationship without first fighting to save it was not a big deal. "Like I said, we'll see. And on that note, I'm gonna have to go." Diamond stood. "Paul and I are going for dinner on South Beach tonight."

Tara stood and walked to the door with her cousin. There, she hugged her. "That's positive. I don't think you guys have done that in a while."

"Nope."

"Then enjoy it, Diamond. And I hope it all goes well when you tell him your good news."

"Me too."

Diamond opened the door and stepped outside. "See you later," she told Tara. "And call Darren."

"I will."

* * *

After checking her cell phone messages, Diamond called Rick at home. She was mildly concerned; his message asking her to call him as soon as possible sounded serious.

Rick answered on the first ring. "Hello?"

"Rick, it's Diamond. Talk to me."

"Diamond, hi. I'm glad you got back to me so quickly."

"What's going on?"

"I dropped by the station earlier today, and I saw Peggy. She told me that she received a letter. At first, she thought it was for anyone, because it was addressed simply to 'DJ.' But when she opened it, she learned it was for you."

Diamond clenched her hand on the steering wheel. "What did it say?"

"There's no other way to tell you this. It was a warning."

"What did it say?" Diamond repeated urgently. Realizing that she'd reached a red light, she slammed on the brakes.

"It read, 'Diamond, watch your back. You've been warned for the last time.' "

Diamond's stomach dropped. "Great."

"There was no postmark. Someone must have dropped the letter off at the station. And we weren't sure how you wanted this handled. We haven't called the police—"

"No. No police."

"Diamond, are you sure? Given the call the other day—"

"Yes, I'm sure. You're forgetting I'm dating a cop. I'll run the scenario by him, see what he says."

"Right. That makes sense."

A horn blared behind her, and Diamond looked up to see the light had turned to green. "Yeah, yeah," she muttered, annoyed. She hit the gas and started to drive. "Listen, I'll see you Monday, okay? But call me in the meantime if anything else comes up."

"You know it."

"And of course, hang on to the letter for me." Even if she didn't truly want to see it.

"Of course."

"Thanks, Rick."

"Later."

Diamond disconnected, then tossed her cell phone onto the passenger seat. "Great. Just great!"

She merged right, heading for the turnpike north, now dreading the dinner with Paul. It would be one thing telling him her good news, but the fact that there was another threat would sour it all.

Another threat. Diamond's stomach tightened with fear.

She'd been anxious to write off the first incident. This one, however, had opened her eyes.

It was the Clay nightmare starting all over again.

Except with Clay, he'd called several times first before progressing to letter writing.

This person had called, then written a letter.

How long before he tried to get up close and personal?

"What's the matter, Diamond?"

Diamond looked up from her plate of food and into Paul's eyes. "Nothing," she lied.

Paul studied her a moment before saying, "You

realize that all you've been doing is nibbling and playing with your food? I thought you were hungry."

"I am." Yet she pushed the plate away. "I was."

"C'mon, Diamond. Tell me what's going on."

Diamond released a shaky breath as she stared at Paul. Here they were, out for the first time in ages, and she should be enjoying herself. Instead, her stomach was a tight mass of mangled nerves—and she wasn't sure she was going to feel any better.

Paul sat back, making a frustrated sound. "I hate when you do this."

"Do what?"

"Shut me out. Damn it, I love you."

"Oh, isn't that sweet." Diamond looked away, toward the right of the patio table where they sat. A steady stream of flashy cars crept along Ocean Drive. Couples and groups of friends strolled on the street along the sidewalk's edge, cut between the cars to get from one side to the other, or howled cheers from their car windows. Everyone was in a festive mood, and she should have been too.

"All right," Paul conceded, raising his hands. "I guess I came on a little strong. But that's because I've felt you slipping away recently. And you have no idea how much that hurts me."

"I'm sorry," Diamond said.

"I don't want to lose you."

Paul reached across the table, extending a hand to her. After a beat, Diamond accepted it.

"The most frustrating thing is that I want to make you happy, but everything I do—like taking you out tonight—seems to blow up in my face. How did we get to this point?"

"I don't know," Diamond replied softly.

Paul ran his thumb along the top of her hand.

"We need to communicate. If we stop talking, stop sharing—we haven't got a fighting chance at saving this relationship."

He was right, and Diamond felt a measure of guilt at how she'd pulled away. How she'd already considered their relationship over, without doing a thing to make it better.

"You might not think that I know you, but I do. And I know that you're keeping something from me. Please, will you tell me what's going on?"

Paul's tone held a hint of desperation, and Diamond's heart cracked. "Yes, I'll tell you. But first, let me say that I haven't told you because I'm afraid of how you'll react." When Paul didn't say anything, she went on. "I've got good news and bad. First"— she couldn't help smiling—"the station has offered my show another time slot because of its popularity."

"I see."

His guarded reaction hurt Diamond. She wanted him to be happy for her. "It'll be a late afternoon slot. They're going to try it for at least a month to see how it goes."

"Well, I never doubted the popularity of your show."

"But you're not happy for me."

"What's the bad news?" Paul asked, ignoring her comment.

While he wasn't expressing elation, at least he wasn't expressing anger, either. And if he had been jumping up and down with joy over her news, Diamond wouldn't buy it.

Still, it would be nice to know that he supported her unconditionally, that what made her happy would make him happy.

Diamond glanced down at the table, then met his eyes again. "I can guarantee you're not going to like this at all. And I only found out a couple hours ago, so it's not like I've been keeping this from you."

Paul's hand tightened around hers. "You're scaring me."

"I . . . there was another threat."

Paul threw his head back and groaned his frustration. "Damn."

"I know. . . ."

"What was it this time?"

"A letter."

"A letter?" Paul's eyes bulged in surprise and concern. "At the station?"

"Yes."

"Was it mailed or hand-delivered—"

"Paul, please stop being a cop and just listen. Let me tell you what it said before you say anything. Please."

Paul nodded tightly.

"It was a letter. And no, it didn't have a postmark, which means someone dropped it off. That's what bothers me the most, that they'd do that. It's just like—"

"Clay."

"Yes," Diamond admitted softly. "That's what this reminds me of."

"So what did the psycho say?"

"The letter said something about a warning. That I'd been warned for the last time. Oh, and the person addressed me as Diamond. Which really bothers me. That's not the name I use on the radio. The guy who called—he addressed me by Diamond. Now this letter addresses me as Diamond."

"Just like Clay."

"Yes. But in many ways, this is more frightening. With Clay, it took him a couple months to progress from calling to writing letters. . . ."

A long, uncomfortable silence passed between them. Finally, Paul said, "I'm worried about you, Diamond."

"I know. I'm worried too."

"Did anyone call the police?"

"I told Rick I'd talk to you first."

Paul nodded. "There are some questions I want to ask Rick. You know what I wish for, but I also know that's expecting a lot. So, the only other option I suppose is that you take extra precautions."

The waiter arrived at their table. "Are you all finished with your dinners?"

"Yes," Diamond replied. "But I'd like to take mine home." It was chicken marsala, her favorite. And while she wasn't hungry right now, she knew she would be later.

"I'm done," Paul said.

"Can I interest either of you in some dessert?"

Both Diamond and Paul seemed to be thinking the same thing, because at that moment, as they looked at each other, both their eyes got that little spark of desire.

"Uh," Diamond began, never taking her eyes from Paul's, "no. You have nothing on the menu that either of us wants."

"Okay, then. I'll be back with your bill."

As the waiter walked off, Paul took Diamond's other hand in his. Then he leaned forward and said, "I can't wait to get you home."

Ten

"Oh," Tara said, unable to hide her disappointment.

"I'm sorry. Believe me, I wish I could see you. But I'm going to be in Sweetwater for quite some time. There's reportedly as much as three feet of flooding because of all the rain. And we haven't even had our first tropical storm of the season yet."

"I didn't realize that you worked weekends."

"Not normally, but I am on call, and if it's really busy and they need me, I go in. It was like that after Hurricane Andrew. Adjusters didn't get any sleep."

Sweetwater was an area in Miami known for its horrible flooding. Tara wondered how anyone continued to live there. Most likely, they couldn't sell their homes if their lives depended on it.

"Then, I have to go into the office for a late meeting. I'm heading out of town."

Disappointment filled her. "You're leaving?"

"Not forever. But I will be gone for four days."

"Oh."

"Convention. So, realistically, the best time for us to get together is next weekend."

Next weekend! Already, Tara missed him.

"I . . ." Her voice trailed off. What could she say?

If the man had work to do, he had work to do. "Well, I guess I'll see you when you get back."

"I guess so."

Tara ended the call with Darren. Then, as she sat moping on the sofa, the phone rang again.

She grabbed it.

"Who am I kidding? I need to see you before I leave."

Darren. Tara's heart melted. "I'd like that."

"It won't be for long, maybe just a quick bite or even a coffee—"

"That'd be fine."

"I'll call you later, then."

"Actually, let me give you my cell number. I think I'll go visit my mother this afternoon, since I haven't seen her in a while."

"Where does she live?"

"Miramar."

"Okay, Broward County. That's not too far."

Tara gave Darren her cell number, and when she ended the call this time, she called her mother and told her she was dropping by. Her mother was pleasantly surprised, and Tara felt a twinge of guilt that she had stayed away so long.

Then she busied herself getting dressed.

But hours later, when she ate dinner with her mother, she still couldn't get her mind off Darren.

Darren's call came close to nine P.M., when Tara was snuggling up on her sofa with a blanket and popcorn, preparing to watch a television movie.

She knew it was him before she even picked up.

"Hey, handsome."

Pause. "Is that how you greet all your male callers?"

"Only the ones named Darren Burkeen."

He chuckled softly. "How did you know it was me? I'm sure the office number doesn't show on your phone."

"I knew it was you."

"Hmm. Maybe you should start one of those psychic phone lines."

"Ha, ha. Very funny." Tara paused. "Are you finally finished for the day?"

"Yep."

Tara's stomach danced with anticipation as she thought of seeing Darren again. But then she realized that perhaps Darren might be too tired to get together, especially if he had to head out of town tomorrow. "If you're too tired to do this, then we don't have to meet."

"No, I'd like to see you. But it can't be for long."

"Any particular place you had in mind?"

"Barnes and Noble has a café."

"That's right," Darren said. "Let's meet there."

Twenty minutes later, Tara pulled into the parking lot of the large Barnes and Noble bookstore on Kendall Drive. Darren had agreed to meet her in the cafeteria, so she went straight there once she headed inside.

When he saw her, his eyes lit up.

A slow breath oozed out of her.

Darren rose to his feet, greeting her with a warm hug. As they pulled apart, Tara's eyes perused his body. He was dressed in black slacks and a form-fitting white cotton top. The man was the epitome of sexy, and he didn't even seem to know it.

"What would you like to drink?" Tara asked. "My treat."

"No, I'll pay." Darren reached into his pants for his wallet.

Tara placed a hand on his wrist, stopping him. "I insist."

"All right, then."

Together, they walked up to the counter. Checking out the menu, Tara asked, "So, what do you want? One of those fancy-schmancy coffees?"

"Naw. I'll take a regular coffee. And a couple of those chocolate chip cookies."

Tara ordered the items, including a fancy coffee with lots of caramel for herself. They went back to their table and sat.

"I really hope you didn't go out of your way to see me," Tara said. Darren looked tired, and she felt a little guilty that he wasn't at home, preparing for bed.

"No, no. I already told you, I wanted to see you."

"Tell me about this convention."

Darren shrugged. "It would bore you."

"No, it wouldn't."

"Sure, it would. Just picture insurance adjusters from across the country all gathered in the same hotel for four days. Insurance adjusters—not mystery novelists. It's all very dry."

Tara giggled. "Not if you all share the kinds of stories you told me."

"It kinda loses its novelty when you see it every day." He sipped his coffee. "Now, your business travel, that must be exciting."

Tara nodded. "Sometimes it is. Just by its nature, of course. I get to travel to different resorts to see what they're like, so I can more effectively sell trips there. It doesn't happen all the time, but enough that it's a nice perk."

"Sounds great."

"It definitely is."

Silence fell between them. Tara couldn't help studying Darren. He seemed different tonight, not like the typical carefree guy he normally was.

"Is something bothering you?" she asked.

"Bothering me?" Darren sat back in his chair. "No. Why?"

"I don't know." Maybe it was her. Maybe she was being paranoid. "You just seem a little . . . preoccupied."

"I guess I am, a little. I'm thinking about the damage I saw today. Sometimes it does get to me, seeing all the tears when people have lost everything. And knowing that whatever dollar figure I come up with will never be enough."

"I can imagine."

They finished their drinks in relative silence, then spent a few minutes perusing the aisle that featured books on travel. Tara showed Darren pictures of some of the places she'd been, and places she'd like to go.

"Truly, though, one of the places I'd love to get to is Africa. West Africa. I want to see where my ancestors came from. It's something I've wanted to do ever since I started celebrating Kwanzaa a few years ago."

"Maybe I'll take you one day."

Tara looked up at Darren. His eyes told her that he was completely serious.

"Maybe," Tara replied softly.

Then Darren yawned, and Tara knew it was time for them to go. "All right, Darren. I won't keep you out any longer."

He glanced at his watch. "Yeah, I better go."

They went to the parking lot, where Darren walked her to her car. Tara unlocked the car and reached for the handle, but Darren quickly put his hand on hers. Slowly, she turned and faced him.

"I apologize that this date was so short," Darren said. "Maybe we can go out to a club next weekend when I'm back. Get our groove on."

He did a silly hip movement, and Tara laughed. "Get our groove on?"

"You know. Dancing."

"Dancing?" Tara asked.

"Yeah," Darren replied. "You do know what that is, don't you?"

Tara placed both hands on her hips and gave Darren a mock-scowl. "Of course I know what dancing is. But don't you remember, I told you I'm not great at it? In fact, I suck."

"You said you couldn't do any of the Latin dances."

"I'm not a dancer, period."

Darren reached for her hand, then stepped back, pulling her away from the car. "Well then, Tara, I'd say it is my duty to teach you." Lifting her arm, he urged her into a twirl. Tara giggled as she completed the dance move—then stopped laughing promptly as she landed against Darren's chest.

He stared down at her, his dark eyes intense. "So? Do we have a date?"

A couple strolled by en route to a car, seemingly oblivious of them.

"Darren . . ." To Tara's surprise, she was suddenly short of breath.

"What? Concerned because people are watching?"

He twirled her again, then lowered her in a dip.

Tara squealed as she went down, though she knew he would never let her fall.

"Are you having fun, Tara?"

"Yes."

"Then say yes. Let's hit the club when I get back. You'll have fun then, too."

The man was entirely too charming, which made it impossible to say no to him. "All right."

"Great."

He lifted her, drawing her body to his. "But I haven't been to a club in ages, so don't expect me to even fit in."

"Then we'll make it an afternoon date. A little more casual." Darren's hands slipped to Tara's waist, and he gently began swaying her from side to side, as though soft music were playing. "Mango's on South Beach has a reggae band on Sunday afternoons."

"Mango's!" Tara exclaimed, startled. "Only model types frequent South Beach."

"Which is exactly why I want to take you there."

With one hand on her waist, Darren took one of Tara's hands in his. Their movements were still slow and rhythmic, as if they were dancing to a Brian McKnight love ballad. Holding her hand, he now led her in a slow turn.

More people passed by, staring at them.

"I can't believe we're dancing in a parking lot!"

"It feels like just the two of us to me."

Tara closed her eyes and laid her head against Darren's chest. She blocked out all thoughts and concentrated only on him, as if they *were* the only two people out here.

"I thought you said you weren't a good dancer," Darren commented.

"I'm not."

Darren pulled back. Tara opened her eyes and looked up at him. He raised an eyebrow in disagreement and said, "Then what do you call what you're doing now?"

"This . . . this is different."

"Different?"

"Yes," Tara replied. "There's no music."

Darren nuzzled his nose against her cheek. "Oh, yes, there is. Don't you hear it? It's our own special song, Tara."

Tara closed her eyes and continued to sway with Darren. He was right. There was music, music that enveloped them as they held each other, even if no one else could hear it. In Darren's arms, Tara felt a sense of sensuality she'd never felt before. And she felt the need to rest her face against his shoulder once more and dance forever to their own special melody. Was he this romantic with every woman he dated? Or just her?

Darren lifted their joined hands to his lips, then kissed hers. "God, Tara. You take my breath away." When she blushed, he added, "You do know how beautiful you are, don't you?"

"I hardly stand around in front of the mirror asking who's the fairest of them all, if that's what you mean."

Darren chuckled. "Beautiful and a sense of humor. Ah, Tara. There's something about you that drives any man with a pulse wild."

Tara stilled. "Except the guy I was supposed to marry. I'm sorry." Darren was a good man. The last thing she should have been doing was crying over Harris when she was in his arms. "I guess I'm not feeling very desirable these days."

"Trust me." Darren framed her face. "You are. If your ex didn't know what he had, then like I said before, he's the fool."

Holding her face, he merely stared at her, and Tara's pulse quickened. The moment stretched until it became agonizing. Her whole body tingled in anticipation of the moment his lips would meet hers.

She watched as his face slowly advanced; then his eyes closed, and her own fluttered shut, the most sensual feeling washing over her.

And then his mouth touched hers, like a brush of silk against her skin. The contact was all too brief, leaving her wanting more. When there was no more, her eyes popped open. She found Darren looking at her.

Despite the fact that they hadn't gone anywhere special, Tara knew she would always cherish this date, this impromptu dancing lesson in the parking lot of the Barnes and Noble.

"All right. I really do have to go now. I'll call you when I get back."

Tara could only stare at him, dumfounded. "That . . . that's it?"

"What—your dancing lesson?" But his smile was mischievous, telling her that he knew exactly what she was referring to.

He was enjoying this game. He wanted to make her weak in the knees with longing, then leave!

"I kind of thought . . . You *are* going to be gone for a week. . . ."

Darren made a face as if he were trying to figure her out but couldn't. Oh, he was playing with her, all right.

"Is there something you want, Tara?"

"Yes," she replied adamantly. She threw her arms around his neck and said, "This."

Tara raised her lips to his, then gave him a good-bye kiss that would have him dreaming of getting back to her as soon as he could.

Eleven

For a casual date, Tara was certainly taking a long time to get ready!

Casual, Darren had said, yet here she was, unable to decide what to wear, what to do with her hair—all that important stuff. And she didn't want to call him back to ask what kind of casual he meant. That would be silly.

It had been almost a week since she'd seen him, and she wanted to look good. She wanted to emphasize to him what he'd been missing while he was away, especially since he'd continued to romance her with cards and flowers twice this week. He made her feel special, so she wanted to look special. But she also didn't want to get dressed in her Sunday best if they were going somewhere that called for jeans.

Once again, she skimmed through all the outfits that hung in her closet. Why couldn't she find anything appropriate? She wasn't a jeans type of girl; that was her problem. Slacks or a skirt was more her everyday style.

"Good grief," she muttered. "You aren't dressing to meet the president." She grabbed a cotton dress with a delicate floral print off a hanger. It was the kind of dress that fit many occasions. With sandals, it was casual. With low-heeled pumps and a shawl, it was more dressy.

If she was a little dressier than Darren, so be it.

The phone rang, and dropping the dress onto the bed, Tara hurried to answer it, wondering if it was Darren.

"Hello?" she said in her best sexy voice.

Nothing.

"Hello?" Tara repeated.

Again, nothing.

Waiting another couple of seconds and hearing no response, Tara replaced the receiver, then scooped up the dress off the bed and went back to the task of getting ready.

For the next half-hour, she applied makeup and lightly curled her shoulder-length hair. Standing back, she looked at her reflection with a satisfied smile.

She looked . . . A smile spread on her face. She looked more beautiful than she could ever remember being.

Okay. I'm ready.

Back in the bedroom, she sat on the edge of her bed and called Darren.

"Hey, beautiful," Darren said when he answered the phone.

Tara was momentarily taken aback at his greeting. Then, she realized that he must have caller ID, and therefore he knew it was her on the line.

"Is that the way you greet every woman who calls you?" Tara teased.

"Only the ones named Tara Montgomery."

Tara smirked. "Well, that's good to hear."

"You ready?"

"Mmm-hmm." Pause. "By the way, did you call here a little while ago?"

"No," Darren answered. "Why?"

"I just wondered. I got a call, but no one said anything."

"If I had called, you know I definitely would've said something."

"Yes, I figured that, but wondered if you'd maybe called from a cell phone and gotten a bad connection. . . ."

"You sound a little concerned. Are you?"

A beat. "I don't know if I should be. I've gotten a few hang-up calls lately."

"Really?"

"Yeah, but it's probably nothing. There's no heavy breathing or anything retarded like that. Just dead air."

"Hmm. Maybe it's the ex." Darren spoke matter-of-factly, but Tara sensed concern in his tone.

"I doubt that. Highly."

"You never know. He may have realized how big a fool he was and wants you back. . . ."

"Oh, yeah." Tara chuckled sarcastically. "Not." But she suddenly couldn't help wondering. What if Harris *was* calling her, but got too afraid to speak once he heard her voice?

What if nothing. Tara wasn't going to waste another moment considering the possibility.

"Anyway," she continued, "I just wanted to let you know that I'm on my way." *And I'm looking forward to it.*

"I hope you're dressed for dancing. . . ."

"I guess I am. . . ." Tara sighed her unease. "Where are you taking me?"

"You'll know soon enough."

"If I'll know soon enough, what's the harm in telling me now?"

"You must be tough to deal with around Christmas," Darren joked.

"Fine," Tara conceded. "I'm on my way."

"See you soon."

Minutes later, Tara was in her car and taking the short drive north to Darren's place.

He lived in a gated community off One-Forty-Seventh Ave, just minutes away from her own apartment complex. Once cleared to pass through the security gate, Tara followed Darren's directions to his house.

Painted in an attractive pale peach, it was the corner unit of a row of town houses. Behind his property, Tara could see the edge of a lake. The thick grass was a vibrant green, and alongside his house, a duck and her ducklings waddled in it.

Tara parked behind Darren's Pathfinder, got out of the car, then walked up to his door. She exhaled a slow breath before pressing the doorbell.

Goodness, she was more nervous than she thought possible! She'd already kissed the man— more than once at that—so what was she afraid of?

It was this whole dating game. It had been so long that Tara didn't know the rules anymore.

So far, she was enjoying the pace of their relationship: slow and easy, getting to know each other and having fun in the process. She wasn't ready to take it to the next level. Yet being here at Darren's house made her wonder if he'd have different feelings in mind, no matter how much of a gentleman he had been thus far.

"Cross that bridge when you come to it," Tara

quietly told herself. Throwing her hand out, she pressed the doorbell.

Seconds later, the door swung open, and Darren greeted her with a warm smile.

"Hey, beautiful."

"Hi." The word escaped her lips on a sigh, because the sight of Darren stole her breath. She couldn't help giving his body a slow once-over. Dressed in a close-fitting black T-shirt and jeans, he made simple look incredibly sexy. No doubt about it, he had an amazing body. Strong, muscular arms and long, lean fingers. She remembered the feel of them wrapped around her body. His wide chest slimmed to a narrow waist. Her eyes ventured lower, to his athletic thighs.

"You coming in?" Darren asked, his sexy voice washing over her like smooth velvet.

Tara's eyes jerked to his face at the question, realizing that she'd been checking him out a little too long. She hoped he hadn't caught her staring!

She straightened her spine, regaining her composure. "Yes. Yes, of course." As Darren held the door open, Tara walked inside. Glancing around, she asked, "You live here alone?"

"Oh, no. My wife's upstairs."

Tara whirled to face him. "What?"

"You set yourself up for that one." Darren flashed her a sly grin. "Of course I live here alone."

Tara cut her eyes at him. "I didn't mean it like that. You could have a roommate—"

"Nope. Just me."

Looking around, Tara said, "It's beautiful." And it was. Elegantly decorated, the house was far different from what she'd stereotypically expect of a single man.

The wide foyer was tiled in a neutral beige. The walls were charcoal gray, which provided a nice contrast to the floor. Two paintings of tropical settings adorned the walls. A square mirror with an ornate wooden frame hung near the door, beneath which was a narrow glass table that rested on a base of granite. On the table were two large candles. Vanilla, Tara realized, judging by the delicate scent that lingered in the air.

"Thank you. I wish I could take credit for it all, but I had a decorator work on the place."

Tara walked farther into the house. The living room furniture was a combination of granite and glass, and sleek black leather. The living room floor was covered in plush white carpet. Off-white vertical blinds were accented with valances that matched the color of the granite.

To the left of the living room, the elegant dining room table rested on tiled floor that matched the foyer's.

The colors of the interior, coupled with the many windows, made the place very bright. Bright was good. Tara loved lots of light.

"Your decorator did a great job. I'd like to—" Tara stopped herself before saying that she'd like to see the bedrooms.

"Like to what?"

"Like to . . . to see the backyard," she finished lamely. "Um . . . I noticed a lake. Does it back onto the water?"

Darren walked to the blinds and pulled the string to slide them open. "Pretty much. It's only about twenty feet away."

Tara crossed the living room and stood beside Darren. "I love the deck. It's a nice touch."

"I built it."

"No way."

"Yep. It was my project when I first moved here three years ago. Too bad I don't get to use it often."

"You spend time building it, yet don't use it?"

Darren shrugged, saying, "I'm a single guy. If I had a girlfriend or a wife, I'd make more use of it."

Tara glanced outside, at the ducks swimming on the water, then back at him, wondering where her relationship with Darren might lead. Would she soon be spending more time here?

Whirling on her heel, she faced Darren again. "So. Where are you taking me?"

Gently, he stroked her chin. "A surprise wouldn't be a surprise if I told you, now, would it?"

"You mentioned going to Mango's in the afternoon, but it's almost evening now . . ."

"You're fishing. And my lips are sealed."

Tara frowned. "All right."

"But we do have to be there by seven, so we've got to get going now."

It was only minutes after five-thirty, which made Tara even more curious as to where they were heading.

Darren took her by the hand. "Come on, beautiful. Let's go."

A little over forty-five minutes later, Tara had her answer. She had known fairly early into the drive that Darren wasn't taking her to Mango's because he'd gone north on I-95 past the exit that would have taken them to South Beach. Now, he pulled his Pathfinder into the parking lot of the Sun Cruz Casino in Fort Lauderdale.

She turned to Darren, her eyes expressing her surprise. "You're a gambler?"

"Me? No, not a chance. A friend of mine coaxed me into going on this cruise once, and it was a lot of fun. And since you mentioned that your ex never took you on a dinner cruise, I figured . . ." His words trailed off, ending with a shrug.

"Oh, Darren." Tara was touched. "I can't believe you remembered that."

"No big deal. It's not a luxury vacation cruise, but I figured it'd be pretty good for an evening. And this way, we can combine a dinner cruise—which you said you wanted to do—with a little fun."

Tara could only stare at him and shake her head.

"What?" he asked, parking the car.

"Oh, I was just thinking that I'd probably make a pretty penny if I could clone you."

Darren raised a dubious eyebrow.

"I'm serious. You almost seem too good to be true."

Darren was silent a moment, as if he were considering her words. Then he said, "Don't make me out to be perfect, Tara. I do have my flaws."

"Like what . . . You're a closet stalker?" Tara suggested, then laughed.

"No, not quite." Pause. "I don't always put the toilet seat down."

"Ooh, how awful. Many women would shoot you for that."

Giving her a wry smile, Darren opened his door and got out. Tara did the same.

"I have to tell you," Tara said, "I rarely gamble because I'm never lucky. I may as well burn a twenty-dollar bill right now."

"Positive thinking, Tara. Where there's a will, there's a way."

"Not when it comes to casinos! They always win."

"Think positive," Darren reiterated. Placing an arm over Tara's shoulders, he led her to the ticket booth to pay for their entry onto the boat.

"There's a great buffet aboard," Darren explained once he'd bought the tickets. "But once the ship sets sail at seven, they clear the food. That's why I figured we should get here a little earlier."

The Sun Cruz Casino was a popular tourist attraction in South Florida, but Tara had never been on it before. She remembered Darren's comment that people often ignored what was in their own backyard, and couldn't help thinking that truer words had never been spoken.

Once they were aboard the boat, the delicious smell of prime rib made Tara's stomach grumble, and reminded her that she'd only had a light breakfast several hours earlier.

"Outside or inside?" Darren asked.

"It's a nice evening. Let's head outside."

Their plates filled, Darren led the way to a table near the boat's railing. Beyond the marina, the view of the water was endless.

Once seated, Tara said, "You didn't tell me. How was your convention?"

"All right," Darren replied simply.

"No interesting tidbits to share?"

"Naw."

Tara watched Darren a moment, but he began eating, effectively ending the conversation. For a moment, she wondered why he didn't have much to say. Given the stories he'd shared with her about his career before, she thought for sure he'd have some interesting things to say about the convention now.

Like Darren, Tara started eating. They both ate in relative silence, and when they were finished, Darren led Tara to the boat's edge. She felt a sudden jerk, then giggled when she realized that the boat was starting to move.

Darren stood behind Tara, placing an arm on either side of her to grip the rails. Tara's breath snagged in her chest at the flood of sensation that rushed through her. She resisted the urge to lean back and rest her head against Darren's strong body.

"So, are you feeling lucky?" Darren asked.

"Yes," Tara replied. "Yes, I am."

"Me too."

Twelve

Darren stared at the back of Tara's head as the boat sailed toward the three-mile point in the ocean that Florida law required it to reach before anyone could start to gamble. The hint of the breeze off the water flirted with her ebony hair, and Darren was doing everything in his power to resist slipping his fingers into the shoulder-length strands.

Her body skimmed his as she gently moved, and Darren wondered if she knew how much the mere brushing of her body against his was turning him on. He closed his eyes, inhaling the delicate floral scent of her perfume. The fragrance seemed uniquely her.

He wanted her, more than he'd wanted anyone.

He'd wanted her from the moment he'd first seen her. Never had Darren had such a reaction to a woman. One look in those beautiful, mesmerizing eyes, and something had told him that she was the one.

In an instant. That's how quickly it had happened.

Until he'd met Tara, he had heard the phrase "love at first sight," but he had never believed in it, much less expected ever to experience it himself. Yet here he was, having fallen for her.

Hard.

He had spent practically every night since he'd met her thinking about her, wondering if she would ever call him, wondering why he couldn't get her off his mind. And the day she'd finally returned his call, he couldn't deny that he felt as if his whole world had changed for the better.

His feelings for her were true. Already, he couldn't imagine spending the rest of his life without her. They had an easy rapport, and that was a definite plus in any relationship.

He knew she hadn't taken his interest seriously. The intensity of his attraction had surprised even him. But he'd always been a straight shooter, and he'd known from the beginning that he couldn't walk away without letting her know how much he liked her.

She turned suddenly, her eyes lighting up as she looked at him. "Thanks so much."

He ached to take her in his arms. "For?"

"For bringing me here. Believe it or not, I've never gone on a cruise. Even though I sell them, I haven't yet been on one. As a travel agent, I can get a greatly discounted price, and I'd always suggested to Harris that we go. But it never happened. So this is . . . nice."

"*Never* been on a cruise?"

"Never."

He raised an eyebrow. "Guess we'll have to rectify that."

Tara gave him a skeptical look.

"You don't believe me, do you?"

Tara shrugged. "I know I want to."

Darren placed a soft kiss on her forehead. "It's a little hard for me to believe, too."

"What do you mean?"

"I mean . . ." Deep breath. "I mean that my attraction for you caught me completely by surprise. I don't know why I feel the way I do. I only know that it's real."

Something flashed in Tara's eyes, something unreadable. Fear? Darren couldn't be sure. She was silent a moment, then turned back to the water.

Darren ran his hands down the length of her arms, then closed his eyes. It was probably best that she turned away.

The thoughts going through his mind scared him. They would no doubt terrify her.

"I *swear,*" Tara began, giggling. "I am *never* lucky."

"I think you can stop saying that now," Darren said over the sound of the coins clanging as they dropped from the slot machine.

"How can this be?" Tara began to gather up the eighty coins that had fallen from the quarter slot machine. "Every machine I've been on tonight has paid me something. Usually, I lose all my money." Tara paused to give Darren a sheepish grin. "Sorry that you're not lucking out. Believe me, I know how it feels."

"Yeah. Sure."

Laughing again, Tara gathered up the last of her coins. "Wow, this cup is getting heavy."

"How awful."

"Shut up," Tara teased.

"You want to go to one of the card tables?"

"Not really. I don't do card games. Besides, I'm on a roll with these machines. But if you want to play blackjack or roulette—"

"Naw, that's okay. Let's ride out your wave."

Tara quickly spun on her heel, scouting for the next machine she felt would be lucky for her. After a while, she stopped in front of a dollar machine. "This one," she said. "I'm getting a good vibe about this one." She glanced at Darren. "Can you spot me a twenty? You know I'm good for it," she added with a sly smile.

Darren dug into his wallet and withdrew a twenty, which Tara placed into the machine.

"What are you waiting for?" Darren asked when she merely sat in the chair, not doing anything.

"I'm trying to decide if I should play the maximum bet." Tara looked up. Above the row of machines, a digital board displayed the figure of four thousand, three hundred, and fifty-five dollars in a variety of flashing colors. "I've won enough money so far that I don't mind gambling a bit more of it." She shrugged. "And I'm still feeling lucky."

"Go for it," Darren said.

That was all the encouragement Tara needed. She pressed the button that said maximum bet, then grabbed the lever and gave it a good tug.

After the first few pulls—and nine dollars of her money—Tara looked up at Darren and said, "I chose this machine because of the diamonds. My cousin is nicknamed Diamond, so I'd hoped this one would be lucky for me." She bit her inner cheek. "I don't know . . ."

"Maybe you shouldn't bet the maximum bet," Darren suggested. "You lose your money that much faster."

Tara shook her head. "I may as well live life on the edge." Then she gave the lever another pull.

For her efforts, she was awarded nine dollars. Not much, but at least she hadn't lost any money.

She looked up at Darren. "You pull it this time."

"All right." Darren moved toward the lever, but before he gripped it, he did a silly motion with his hands, as though he were weaving a magic spell on the machine.

Tara giggled at his silliness.

Darren curled his fingers around the lever, then looked at Tara. "Are you ready?"

Tara smiled. "Do it."

Darren did, and after a beat, the slot machine started spinning. Round and round the icons went.

Diamond.

Diamond.

Diamond.

Bells started to ring at the same time that Tara started to squeal with delight. "Oh my God!" she exclaimed. "Oh my God!"

Darren stared at the machine with a mix of wonder and disbelief. It took a few seconds for it to dawn on him that not only had they hit the jackpot, they'd been playing the maximum bet.

That meant they'd won the progressive prize.

Four thousand, three hundred, and fifty-five dollars.

"We won!" he finally shouted.

Besides the flashing lights and ringing bells, there was a sudden buzz of excitement around them. People were gathering to see what had happened, just how lucky they'd been. Then a member of the Sun Cruz Casino staff was pushing his way through the crowd. That's when it really hit Darren that this wasn't a joke.

"Congratulations," the manager said. He shook Darren's hand.

"Just confirm this for me," Darren said cautiously. "Did we really just win over four thousand dollars?"

"You sure did." The manager beamed an ear-to-ear smile.

Hearing his words, Tara grabbed Darren by the hands and squeezed. "Darren, I swear—"

"I know, I know. You never win."

Tara could only nod to indicate that that was what she was going to say.

"You definitely have to stop saying that now." Darren draped an arm across her shoulder. "Because tonight, you've officially ended that nonwinning streak."

Later, Darren and Tara were still beaming.

After their big win, they had wisely decided to stop gambling for the night. Neither of them had expected to walk away with any money, so to have a couple extra thousand dollars each in their pockets was a pure bonus.

And for Tara, it was a bonus on top of what had turned out to be an incredible evening spent with Darren.

Now, in the doorway of his home, she looked up at him. The night sky framed his body; the moon cascaded its rays upon them both. Crickets sang in the darkness, but the rest of the world seemed still.

As she stared up at him, Tara didn't know if he was going to kiss her or not. She only knew that she wanted him to.

"I had a really, really great time tonight," Tara told him.

"Of course you did. You kept winning and winning. For any gambler, that chalks up to a great night."

Tara playfully swatted his arm. "That's not what I mean."

Darren slipped an arm around her waist and urged her closer to him. "It isn't?"

Something changed between them then. The air between them seemed to crackle with electricity. "No."

"Then what do you mean?" Darren's voice was a whisper.

"I had a great time tonight . . . because of you."

"That makes two of us."

There was a pause. Then Tara said, "Well, I guess I should be going."

Darren's fingers played on the small of her back. "You don't have to."

Butterflies tickled Tara's stomach. She should have expected this offer. "I . . . No, I think I should just go home."

"I guess that came out wrong." Darren moved his hands forward, to her hips, taking a small step backward as he did. "It wasn't an invitation to go to bed."

Maybe not, but with the way he was touching her, and the way she felt in his arms, it wouldn't be long before the two of them ended up making love. The very thought made Tara nervous. She suddenly realized that she wasn't ready for the next step.

Given how the day had gone, it certainly wasn't crazy to expect it might lead to sex. But she was still getting to know him, and she wasn't ready to do something that she might later regret.

"If I come in, we'll be setting ourselves up for—"

Tara stopped when Darren pulled her close once again, his face already lowering to hers. She didn't have time to protest before his lips came down on hers, softly, sweetly. Surprise melted into surrender.

Unexpectedly, Darren pulled away, and Tara gave a soft moan of protest.

Darren looked into her eyes and said, "I'm in love with you, Tara."

Tara froze. As she looked up at Darren, trying to read his eyes, it seemed as if a hundred years passed.

Had she heard him correctly? Had he just said that he was in love with her?

"Yes," Darren stated, answering her unspoken question. "It's true. I know it seems crazy, but I am in love with you."

Tara took a cautious step backward, away from him. Her body came to rest against his front door. A nervous giggle escaped her. "How can you be in love with me? You've known me what—a month? That doesn't make any sense."

"I know it's been quick—"

"Quick? That's the understatement of the year."

Darren exhaled softly. "If you want to know the truth, I fell in love with you the moment I saw you."

Tara laughed. "Come on."

"I'm not lying about this, Tara. I didn't believe in love at first sight either—until you."

"Darren." Tara merely stared at him. He met her eyes with a steady gaze, and the fact that she saw only truth in his eyes scared her to death.

She turned away. "This . . . I . . . I don't know what to say."

"I know what I'd like you to say." Darren's tone was gentle. "Of course, I don't expect that." He paused. "I don't know why I told you how I feel. I figured it would frighten you, so I hadn't planned on sharing that with you—yet. I guess I just wanted you to know that if you came inside and we *did* end up in bed, it wouldn't just be sex. It would be about love."

About love? Tara faced him again. She was barely out of a long-term relationship with a man she'd planned to marry.

She wasn't ready for love from someone else.

This was too much to deal with. She couldn't handle Darren's confession.

"Darren, I . . . I have no idea what to say. This is . . . it's too much." She took a few side steps until she was no longer in front of him. "I'm going to have to talk to you later."

"Tara." Darren reached for her arm.

But she shrugged him off and hurried to her car, digging her key out of her purse as she did.

She got into her car and sped off, trying to forget the fact that Darren was standing at the end of his driveway, helplessly watching her run away.

Thirteen

Four days later, Tara hadn't returned any of Darren's calls. He had left several messages, but she didn't know what to say to him.

Staring down at the mountain of folders on her desk, Tara inhaled a deep breath. She pulled off her telephone headset and tossed it on her desk, then dragged a hand over her face. What *could* she say to him?

Darren had dropped a bomb on her, one that had changed everything.

One minute they were getting to know each other; the next, he had skipped the several stages that should follow in slow progression on the road to getting seriously involved—like going from A to Z without the in-between.

Tara wasn't prepared for Z.

She liked him, yes. She enjoyed their time together, yes.

But love?

Darren's admission had made it impossible for them to continue casually dating. The more time they spent together, the more he would want from her. It would now be an unspoken fact that if she continued to date him as she had been, she was accepting that the relationship was suddenly serious.

It would have been one thing to continue dating if Tara hadn't known he was in love with her. But she did, and that meant she should not lead him on.

Would not.

Diamond had understood her concern. Her cousin had wisely suggested that she at least take some time to herself to think. "He seems nice enough," Diamond had said. "But in case he's one of those cling-on type guys, you need to take a breather now and see if he understands, or if he freaks. Some of those nice guys have a dark side."

Tara hadn't been concerned about that. Not that Diamond's words of caution weren't wise, but that wasn't the sense she got from Darren.

Frustrated over the whole situation, Tara closed her eyes. When she opened them and sat up straight, she was startled to find a compact mirror in front of her face. Her gaze jumped from the mirror to the person who held it.

Sharnette shook her head as she stared down at her.

"God, you totally scared me," Tara complained.

"Well, someone has got to do something to help you snap out of this depression."

"I'm not depressed."

"Girl, who are you trying to fool? Didn't you see that frown on your face?" Sharnette placed her hands on her hips. "You should have at least slept with him."

"Sharnette, not now." This was one time Tara was not in the mood for her friend's joking nature.

"I know, I know. You think I'm being insensitive."

Instead of dropping the issue, Sharnette rounded the desk, resting her butt against it as she got closer to Tara. "But the truth is, if you had slept with him, it would've been about sex, about putting Harris out of your mind. Instead, you treated this like a relationship. Now, everything is more complicated."

"I wasn't looking for a roll in the hay. I wanted to spend time with someone who was nice, who was a potential . . ." Tara's voice trailed off.

"But you weren't ready for that."

"No, I guess not."

Her phone rang then. Glad for the diversion, Tara quickly grabbed the receiver. "Wholesale Travel, Tara speaking."

"Hello," came the faint reply.

"How may I help you?"

Pause. Then, "Where's Diamond?"

"Excuse me?"

Click.

Tara held the receiver away from her face, staring at it in confusion. Someone had called for her cousin? Why?

"Who was that?" Sharnette asked.

"I don't know." Tara replaced the receiver. *That was weird.*

"I know you think I'm interfering in your private life," Sharnette began, "but we've been friends for a long time—"

"Sharnette, you know I love you. But this is something I have to deal with on my own. It really doesn't help when you joke with me about it, even though I know you mean well."

"I'm sorry. In my own weird way, I've been trying to be there for you."

"I understand. It's okay."

"You want some sincere advice?" Sharnette asked. She didn't give Tara a chance to say no. "Maybe he truly is one of the nice guys. I mean, does it make him crazy because he fell for you so quickly? If I were you, I would tell him that you need a little more time. Then you can decide where you want to go from there. But that means you have to call him. You can't ignore him forever."

"I guess that's a good idea."

"Then do it, Tara. Don't put it off a moment longer."

It was near the end of the day that Tara was struck with the sense of déjà vu. Looking up when the door chimes sang, she saw a huge arrangement of flowers.

"Tara Montgomery?" the deliveryman asked. He was one she hadn't seen here before.

Tara slowly rose from behind her desk. "That's me."

"These are for you."

The man walked toward her. The bouquet consisted of pink and white carnations, baby's breath, and tiny red roses. It was simply beautiful.

The man placed the flowers on her desk. Tara's heart skipped a beat.

Darren.

Tara reached for her purse, and gave the deliveryman a tip. As soon as he turned away, Tara took the card from the floral arrangement and read it.

I'm sorry I scared you. But I meant what I said.
Please call me. I miss you.
Darren

Tara felt the fight go out of her. Maybe she was being too hard on him. Maybe if she called him and explained that she needed to take things slowly, everything would be fine.

She wanted no strings attached, at least at this point. She knew how it felt to have her heart broken. That was the last thing she wanted to do to Darren.

Yes, she decided. She would call him. Tonight. When she got home.

It was raining by the time Tara arrived home, and she had to run from her car and to her apartment door as fast as she could to avoid getting drenched. She'd lived in Florida all her life and known how suddenly the weather changed in the summer, yet she was caught without her umbrella more times than she cared to remember.

Her phone was ringing when she opened her door. Hurrying inside, Tara tossed her purse onto the nearby sofa and ran to answer the phone.

"Hello?"

"Put Diamond on the phone," a gruffy voice said.

"Diamond?"

"You heard me."

Tara frowned. "Who is this?"

The caller hung up.

Replacing the receiver, Tara couldn't help wondering what was going on. First the call for her cousin at her workplace today. Now this?

And it concerned her that with both calls, she hadn't been able to discern if the voice belonged to a man or a woman.

Lord help her, was it another stalker?

Tara had the eerie feeling that both calls had to do with the one Diamond had gotten at the radio station.

But if it was someone else who now had his sick sights on Diamond, how did he know about Tara? And worse, how did he know where she lived and worked?

A chill snaking down her spine, Tara wrapped her arms around her torso.

Then she whirled around and snatched up the receiver. She needed to call her cousin. Let her know what was going on. She dialed her cousin's number. Paul answered almost immediately.

"Hey, Paul. Is Diamond there?"

"Tara?"

"Yes, it's me."

"No, she's not here. She's at the station."

"That's right. I forgot about her new time slot."

"You can try her on her cell phone if you need to reach her right away. But I'll give her the message that you called."

"Thanks, Paul. Take care."

Tara called her cousin's cell the moment she hung up with Paul. Her voice mail picked up immediately. Tara left her a brief message asking Diamond to call her as soon as she could. The calls she'd received were too bizarre to ignore; Tara was definitely concerned.

With the receiver back in place, Tara's hand lingered on the phone. It was at a time like this that she most missed having a man in her life. She would certainly feel safer with a man around, or at least one in her life she could call.

Her mind drifted to Darren. Should she call him now?

Instead of lifting the receiver, Tara went to the sofa and sat down. Her gaze going to the window, she watched the rain as it came down in heavy sheets.

The rain reminded her of evenings with Harris, evenings spent curled up on the sofa, cuddling and watching a movie.

Harris . . .

His name sounded softly in her mind, and she sighed.

Was that her problem where Darren was concerned? That she couldn't forget Harris?

She hated to admit it, but a part of her still missed him. Not every day, and not because she still wanted a relationship with him. But every now and then, when something would remind her of the kind of thing they'd do together, she did miss what they had shared.

But when would she stop missing him altogether? The man had gone and done the unthinkable, and for her to waste even a moment's thought on him . . .

But that was so much easier said than done.

He was a fool. Darren's words about Harris sounded in her mind.

It was, truly, as simple as that, wasn't it? She'd been with Harris for five years; she'd always been a patient and loving girlfriend, and she knew she would have made a good wife.

And then Harris up and got engaged to someone else.

It was simple, yet complicated. She supposed what she really wanted was to hear from him, even now. She wanted to hear the truth from his own lips—but he didn't even have the decency to do that.

Forget Harris, she told herself sternly.

A weary sigh escaped her as she remembered Darren's note. She missed him, too. And she wanted to call him, to at least be as honest with him about her feelings as he had been with her. If that honesty was the end of their friendship, then it wasn't meant to be.

After sitting and debating the issue for several minutes, Tara jumped to her feet. Needing a diversion from her thoughts, she headed to the kitchen, where she searched her fridge for food.

Nothing.

Her stomach churned, but it wasn't from hunger. She was still thinking of Darren, and the thought of calling him still scared her.

Just call him.

Steeling her nerves, Tara headed for the living room phone. She punched in Darren's home number.

Then held her breath as she waited.

After four rings, his voice mail came on.

Great, she thought. She'd gotten up the nerve to call him, all for nothing.

She did the only thing she could do. She left him a voice message.

All she could do now was wait.

Tara didn't have to wait long. Less than twenty minutes later, her phone rang.

"Hello?"

"Tara," came the cautious reply.

Darren. Tara was surprised at the way her heart fluttered at the familiar sound of his voice.

"Hey," she said, a smile touching her face. "I got your flowers. Thanks."

"You read the card?"

"Yes. And I want to say—"

"Wait," Darren interjected. "I need to tell you this. I know I scared you, Tara. And I didn't want to do that. I'm sorry. But I miss you already. I miss what we shared."

"When you talk like that . . . it scares me." Tara sighed. "I don't want to lead you on. I don't want to hurt you. Yes, I like you, but I'm coming out of a five-year relationship, and I don't know that I'm ready for another one."

"I'm not asking for more than you can give."

"It's not that simple, Darren. When you told me how you feel, that changed everything. I wanted to take things nice and slowly, one day at a time."

"We can still do that."

He was saying all the right things. "You say that now . . ."

"I mean it. Tara, I know that a good thing doesn't need to be rushed. And anything worth having, I can wait for."

"And what if I decide . . . what if I decide that things aren't working out between us? You're going to be hurt."

"That won't be your problem." Darren paused. "I just want to see you. Spend more time with you. I know you're afraid, but I want to assure you that I would never hurt you."

Somehow, Tara knew she could believe him. But she wasn't simply concerned about being hurt; she didn't want to hurt him.

"Do you have any time tonight?"

She felt a jolt in her heart. "Tonight?"

"For dinner?"

"I . . . I guess. I haven't eaten."

"Great."

She could hear a smile in his voice.

"You want to come over? I can cook you some dinner," he said.

Tara glanced outside. The rain had stopped. "Actually, I think we should probably meet somewhere. Considering."

"Sure. That makes sense."

They discussed a place to meet, and minutes later, Tara was getting ready.

She felt better. All she'd needed to do was talk to him and explain how she felt. Now, she was assured that Darren wouldn't pressure her, which was what she'd needed.

For the first time in a long time, Tara smiled.

Fourteen

The rain started up again about an hour later, when Tara was ready to leave her apartment. This time, the rain was accompanied by heavy winds. As Tara peered through her bedroom window at the downpour, she couldn't help wondering if there was a storm coming. Thus far, the news reports hadn't mentioned anything about a possible hurricane, but it wouldn't be the first time a sudden storm erupted, bringing with it lots of water that could easily flood some areas by morning if the rain didn't let up.

Her phone rang. Sitting on the edge of the bed, she grabbed the receiver from the night table.

"Hello?"

"Tara, it's me."

"Hi, Darren." She glanced at the clock. "Everything okay?"

"Actually, I have to cancel. I got beeped. I have to go out to an MVA."

"A what?"

"A motor vehicle accident."

Tara's stomach dropped in disappointment. "Oh."

"I'm not sure how long I'll be. Maybe we can get a bite to eat later?"

"I guess. Will you call me when you know you're free?"

"Of course." Pause. "Sorry."

"Don't be sorry. It's not your fault."

"I'll call you as soon as I can."

"Good-bye. Oh, and—" Tara stopped talking when she heard the dial tone in her ear.

Be careful, she finished silently.

Tara replaced the receiver, then lay back. A long sigh oozed out of her.

But then she smiled. This little setback had proven one thing to her: She missed Darren, and she was definitely looking forward to seeing him again.

The pounding on her door startled Tara awake. Slowly rising, she listened to make sure she'd heard correctly.

More urgent pounding.

Tara hopped off the bed and hurried to the front door. A quick look through the peephole told her it was Diamond. Tara unlocked the door and opened it. Diamond breezed past her into the apartment.

"Diamond . . ."

"Tara, I don't know what's happening."

Tara very rarely saw her cousin lose her composure, and this was one of those rare times.

"Diamond, my God. You look . . . you actually look pale." Which was a hard thing for the dark-skinned beauty to accomplish.

"I didn't tell you. I got another letter at the station nearly two weeks ago."

"What?"

"I know. . . . I guess I was hoping that by ignoring it, it would go away. But this isn't stopping, Tara. Today, he called me at work. And when I went outside to get some fresh air, I saw something on my car. It was an envelope, and inside, a card was ripped to shreds."

Tara approached her cousin, took her by the hands, and led her to the sofa. Together, they sat.

Diamond blew out a shaky breath. "I don't know if I can deal with this again."

"So, you got another letter a couple weeks ago?"

"Yes."

"And you told Paul about it?"

"Yes. And he's worried. But to my surprise, he didn't tell me to quit the show."

"Okay."

"Someone delivered the letter in person, and it reminded me of when Clay had started to get crazier. I worried, but put it out of my mind until today. He knows my car, Tara. How can he know that? I . . . I feel as helpless as I did when Clay was stalking me. God."

Tara rubbed her cousin's back in comfort. "I don't want to worry you more," she said after a moment, "but I got a couple of weird calls today."

Diamond's head shot up.

"Yes," Tara said. "One at the office, and one when I got home."

"Here?" Diamond used a finger to indicate the apartment.

"Here."

Several seconds passed before either of them spoke.

"What am I going to do?"

"Have you contacted the police?"

"No." Diamond shook her head. "You remember how useless they were when Clay was stalking me. They could only react, not do anything to prevent."

"The stalking laws are pathetic," Tara commented. "But they need to know about this."

"Paul knows. When it gets worse—" Diamond stopped abruptly. "Damn, it's already gotten worse. This creep is calling you." She closed her eyes, then reopened them. "Paul is going to want me to quit for sure now."

"Maybe you should consider taking some time off."

Diamond was quiet as she considered Tara's words. Then, her head jerked back and forth in a quick motion. "I can't. Just the thought of it makes me depressed."

"I'm not saying to quit—"

"What if the station thinks I'm too much of a risk? First Clay, now some other loser? No. I won't take any time off. That's letting this jerk run my life, and I refuse to do that."

"But you will go to the police?"

"Yes. Yes, I will."

"Do you want me to go with you?"

"Would you?"

Tara's lips curled in a soft smile. "Of course. How could you even ask?"

By the time Tara left the North Miami Police Department, the streets were starting to flood in some areas. She drove carefully, her mind on two people as she did.

Diamond. And Darren.

She felt a little better about Diamond's situation,

now that she had filed a report with the police. Her cousin would let them know of any other developments. Diamond had felt better by the time she left the police station, heading for the radio station and her late-night show.

Darren . . . As Tara drove along the Palmetto Expressway, she hoped he was okay. He had told her that he'd gone to the scene of an accident, and given the weather, Tara could only assume it was a bad one.

Had someone died?

The very thought made Tara's stomach flutter with fear. She hoped Darren was all right.

And she was also more curious about him than ever. How could a man deal with tragedies on a regular basis, yet still have a positive disposition?

Tara smiled softly. She hoped he finished with his work soon. She definitely wanted to see him tonight.

The sound of the ringing phone jarred Tara awake. A quick glance at her bedside clock told her it was eleven minutes after ten.

Tara reached for the receiver and brought it to her ear. "Hello?"

Silence.

"Hello?" Tara repeated. Again, she was met with silence. Aggravated, she repeated herself, though in an annoyed tone. "Hello."

More silence.

Then, *click*.

Tara let the receiver slip from her ear to her jawline. For several seconds, she sat in silence, with confusion and fear swirling through her.

In the past, she'd simply dismiss such a call as a

prank and let it go. But tonight, she could not help wondering if there was more to the call.

No one had asked for Diamond this time, but that didn't mean this call had nothing to do with her cousin.

Tara lay back and groaned. The whole nightmare with Clay had been one that rocked the sense of security in the Montgomery family. But once it had been resolved, everyone had been hopeful that there would not be a repeat scenario.

Now, only a couple of short years later, here was another troubling situation to deal with.

It was hard to fight a ghost.

Which is exactly what Clay had been, until he'd shown up outside the radio station and attacked Diamond.

There were bound to be harmless lunatics out there—the type who would harass you with calls and letters, but never cross the line to physically hurting you. The problem was, how did you know the difference?

And what did you do to protect yourself?

Just thinking about it, and the endless horrific possibilities, was enough to make anyone crazy. Tara could completely understand why Paul was so concerned, why he pointed out all the worst scenarios to Diamond.

Tara knew her cousin well enough to know that she'd never give up her job. So that left one option: Diamond had to be able to protect herself in case the worst did happen.

But how did you protect yourself from a faceless threat?

When the phone rang again, Tara paused. She

contemplated ignoring it, but after the third ring she snatched the receiver.

"Listen, you might get your thrills out of calling and harassing people—"

"Whoa, hold up, Tara."

"Darren?"

"Yes, it's me."

Tara's shoulders drooped with relief. "Oh, God. I'm sorry."

"What's going on?" Darren asked, concern lacing his tone.

Tara paused. "Oh, nothing really."

"Don't tell me that." Darren spoke firmly. "You don't answer the phone like that if there's nothing going on."

Tara exhaled loudly. "Remember that night when I asked if you'd called me and hung up? Well, I'm still getting some strange calls. Two today. And my cousin came over all upset; she thinks someone may be harassing her."

"I'm coming over."

"You don't have to."

"This person called minutes before I called, right?"

"Yes," Tara replied.

"Then I don't want to take any chances. You live alone, right?"

"Yes."

Tara could not say anything else before Darren asked for her address. She gave it to him.

"Great," Darren said after confirming the address. "I'm heading right over. And don't worry, Tara. I just want to come over and make sure that you're safe. If your phone rings again, let me answer it. That way, if someone is bothering you, they'll realize that you are not alone, and that will hopefully deter them."

Tara inhaled deeply, then exhaled. His idea actually made sense. "Okay."

"I'll see you soon."

Something was wrong with her.

Because the moment Darren walked through her door and swept her into his arms, Tara's mind ventured to sex.

Every part of him filled her senses. His musky scent was distinctly masculine. The feel of his hard body against her soft one made her even more sexually aware. The sound of his urgent breathing, like he'd rushed to her apartment to make sure she was okay, filled her with the sweet sensation of what it was like to have a man protecting you.

And of course, he was beautiful. The sight of him dressed in a long black trench coat when she opened the door instantly set her pulse racing. He oozed strength and power.

"Are you okay?"

A beat. "Yes."

"He didn't call again?"

"No one called."

Darren's hand went to her head, and he gently ran a hand over her hair. Good Lord, if she could stop time, she would. This moment was ripe with glorious sensations, and Tara wanted to savor it always.

Darren pulled back and looked into her eyes. "I'm sorry if it seems I overreacted. It's just that . . . when I care, I care. I don't want to see anything bad happen to you."

"No need to apologize." Her lips curled in a soft smile. "Actually, it's nice to feel this cared for."

The truth was, Tara couldn't imagine Harris high-tailing it to her apartment just because she'd gotten a call that had unnerved her. He'd try to make her feel better over the phone, and he'd tell her to let him know if the person called again.

But this—Darren's reaction—was exactly what she wanted. There was something thrilling about a man taking charge this way, not letting anything get in the way of his attempts to protect her.

"Well, come in." Tara giggled as she stepped backward. She brushed her hands over her silky robe, for the first time realizing that she was wet from the rain on Darren's coat.

"I got you all wet. Sorry."

A frisson of hot energy shot through her body, thinking of the double meaning of Darren's words. Whoa, what was wrong with her?

Nothing, she realized. Nothing at all. She was still a woman, a woman with desires and needs.

And Darren was one helluva man.

After Harris, Tara had lost her sexual drive—but boy had it returned now with full force!

"Why are you looking at me like that?" Darren questioned.

"Huh?" How was she looking at him?

Darren's eyes darkened, and Tara saw his chest rise and fall with a slow and steady breath. "I wanted to make sure you were safe, but . . ."

"But what?"

"But maybe I should go."

Pause. "Why?"

"Because . . . something's different about you to-night." He frowned as he studied her. "And I can't help but remember what you said the last time, about what you didn't want. . . ."

Tara felt a surge of sexual power. "What did I say?"

Darren chuckled uncomfortably. "Come on. You know what I'm talking about."

Tara took a step toward him, not sure what had gotten into her. She only knew that she was enjoying every minute of flirting with him. "Uh-uh. Why don't you spell it out?"

Darren's eyes narrowed as she closed the distance between them. His mouth fell open, as though he wanted to say something, but no words came out when Tara slipped her arms around his neck.

Finally, he sputtered, "Wh-what are you doing?"

Her bravado crumbled a bit, and she let out a nervous breath. "Honestly? I don't know."

She let her hands fall away from Darren's neck. Darren quickly reached out and snagged her wrist.

He said, his voice deep with emotion, "I didn't say that you had to stop."

Tara stepped toward him again, her body molding to his. Her hands slipped beneath his coat, gently skimming his body. Bringing them higher, she let her fingers play over his pecs, enjoying the feel of his hard muscles.

Slowly, she trailed her fingers upward, once again resting them at the nape of his neck. When she looked up, Darren eyes instantly met her gaze. The next instant, his mouth covered hers ferociously.

Tara mewled against his lips, her eyes fluttering shut.

Darren wrapped his arms around her waist, pulling her closer as his tongue slipped into her mouth. Though he held her lightly, Tara was distinctly aware of the touch of each of his fingers through the fabric of her robe.

Darren's fingers teased her, sending delightful sensations washing over her. How would it feel if his hands were actually on her skin? Suddenly, Tara wanted the robe gone. She wanted no restrictions between them.

She wanted to make love to him.

But with a groan, Darren pulled away.

Startled, Tara looked up at him, her chest heaving with each ragged breath.

"Tara—"

"No." Tara placed a finger on Darren's lips to hush him. "I don't want to talk."

"I don't want you to do something you're not ready for."

"I am ready—"

"The last time I saw you, you weren't. . . ."

Not quite knowing where she was getting her boldness from, Tara placed a hand at the top of her robe, her fingers teasing the folds. "A woman's entitled to change her mind, isn't she?"

Darren's eyes lingered on her fingers for a few seconds, before rising to meet her eyes. "I may be a gentleman, but I'm still a man. I can only take so much temptation."

"So you're tempted."

"What man in his right mind wouldn't be?"

Tara felt a surge of feminine power at the slight sound of desperation in Darren's tone. Oooh, she was enjoying this. Teasing was definitely fun.

Giving him a coy look, she asked, "Why resist me?"

Then she loosened the tie of her beige robe, revealing the matching beige silk camisole and shorts beneath. As Darren's hot gaze swept over her, she finally admitted to herself that she'd had sex on the brain long before he'd come over. When was the last time she'd worn this sexy ensemble?

Not in ages.

She stepped cautiously toward him.

Darren met her eyes, giving her an intense look. "You told me you weren't ready for this."

"You know, Darren. I think you doth protest too much."

There was a pause; then Tara giggled to lighten the mood. Darren did as well. When the laughing died down, Tara once again put her arms around him. "I'm ready now," she whispered. "Believe me, Darren, I want you."

Fifteen

Darren groaned as he stepped toward Tara, then enveloped her in his arms. In a flurry of motions, Tara stripped Darren out of his overcoat; he stripped her out of her robe. Their hands were on each other again, hot and desperate, pulling at each other's clothes, slipping beneath fabric to touch each other's skin.

Tara sighed her satisfaction when Darren's warm hands skimmed her belly, then went upward slowly, nearing her breasts. Her entire body was alive with sweet anticipation. She held her breath, waiting.

His fingers moved from side to side, not upward as she so craved. Clearly, he knew how to tease as well.

"Oh, Darren . . ."

Finally, his fingers trailed upward to the fullness of her breast. Her body quivered in response. She loved the feel of his hands on her, but this wasn't enough. She needed more.

Tara literally ached for him touch her nipple. Placing a hand on his arm, she guided his hand higher, and after an agonizing moment, the warmth of his palm covered her. Her nipple hardened in response.

"Mmm . . ."

"You like that?" Darren asked.

"Oh, yes."

He stroked his thumb over the peak. "I love the contrast. Soft and hard."

"I need you," Tara said, her breath ragged.

Darren brought his hands to her face, framing it, then lowered his mouth to hers. The kiss was gentle and brief, but made her head light with desire nonetheless.

"The bedroom," Tara said, realizing that they were still in the entranceway of her apartment.

Darren chuckled. "Yeah, that'd be a good idea."

Tara took his hand in hers and led him through the apartment to her bedroom door. When she was about to cross the threshold to her room, Darren stopped.

Tara turned, looking up at him with curious eyes.

"I just want to . . ." Darren paused. "Are you sure? I want you to be sure." Darren was quite positive that most men didn't fight sex the way he was right now, but his feelings for Tara were sincere, and he wanted this to be a step toward strengthening their relationship. He wanted there to be no regrets.

Tara's beautiful face lit up in the sweetest of expressions. Reaching for him, she palmed his face. "Of course I'm sure."

As she looked up at him with those beautiful brown eyes, her full lips slightly parted, Darren wrapped his arms around her and pulled her soft body against his with an urgent tug. The little sound that escaped her indicated her surprise. But the next instant, she was molding her body to his, running her hands over him.

His mouth on hers, Darren led her into the bedroom. She walked backward while he moved forward.

When her legs hit the bed, Tara faltered, and she stumbled backward. Darren tightened his grip around her waist while shooting his other hand onto the bed to brace himself, making sure he didn't crush Tara as they both went down.

Both he and Tara laughed as they bounced lightly on the mattress; then the laughing simultaneously changed to moans, and Darren captured her lips for another hot and hungry kiss.

Tara hurriedly undid the buttons on his shirt. Darren played with the straps on her camisole, pulling them off her shoulders. He kissed the warm flesh of one shoulder, and felt hot desire spread through him at the way she moaned her pleasure. When Tara's hands went to his pants, fumbling with the belt, Darren stood upright. He slipped out of his shirt, undid his belt and button, then let his pants drop to the floor.

Lying on the bed, her black hair spilling around her face, Tara simply watched him. Pale moonlight pierced the darkness of the bedroom, covering her body in a pale glow. Darren's breath caught in his throat. She looked so incredibly beautiful.

I love you. The words sounded in his mind, but Darren resisted saying them. He was still trying to understand how he had come to be so strongly attracted to her in such a short time. He only knew that he had. And as he stared down at her, at the small mound of her breasts beneath her silk and lace camisole, he knew that what he felt for her was different from what he'd ever felt for anyone else. Stronger.

Her eyes on his, Tara slowly rose to her knees on the bed. She pulled the camisole over her head and tossed it onto the floor. Then she slipped her fingers beneath the waistband of her silky shorts and urged them over her hips. Lying back, she dragged the shorts down the length of her legs, then kicked them onto the floor.

It was the most erotic thing Darren had ever seen.

Naked on the bed, Tara stretched out her hands, beckoning to him.

Darren's breath caught in his throat. She truly was the most beautiful woman he had ever seen.

Quickly, he stripped out of his own briefs, then joined Tara on the bed. They lay on their sides, face-to-face, their mouths so close Darren could feel the heat of her breath on his face.

He ached to take her lips in a tender kiss, a kiss that would convey to her the depth of his feelings.

But he knew a kiss like that would lead to an explosion of passion, and in no time he would be inside her. He wanted that, yes, but first, he wanted to explore her body.

He ran his hand down her, barely touching her flesh. Down her arm. Forward, then down, to the groove of her hip. Along her hip's curve. Behind to her buttocks.

Little moans escaped her with each touch. It was too much to handle. Darren could no longer resist pulling her toward him. He devoured her mouth in a hot, frenzied kiss.

Tara draped an arm around Darren's neck and urged him closer, while at the same time turning so that she was on her back. There was no denying it; she needed this. Badly. She needed his mouth all over her skin.

She needed him inside her.

Darren broke the kiss and lowered his lips, planting feathery kisses along her collarbone and up to her ear. The light touch of his mouth on her skin was so provocative, it made her delirious with need.

"Oh," Tara moaned. Darren dipped his tongue into her ear, and heat pooled at the center of her thighs.

His hands explored her body, palming her breast, tweaking a nipple. Tara's body was taut, almost ready to explode.

And when Darren lowered his head and took her nipple in his mouth, gently suckling the hardened peak, Tara's body jerked from the pleasure. Never before had she come so close to climaxing without her womanhood being touched.

She couldn't stand much more of this.

"Darren, I need you."

He kissed a path to her navel, then rose from her body. Tara looked at him in surprise.

"I have to get a condom," he explained.

He fumbled with his pants, and Tara heard the sound of the condom wrapper tearing.

"Let me put it on," she said, her voice husky.

She got on her knees and moved toward the edge of the bed. Darren passed her the package, and she withdrew the condom. She felt the length of his erection first, slowly, and Darren moaned. Then, using both hands, she rolled the condom on.

Once again, she lay back on the bed, this time opening her legs for him. Darren paused only a moment before lowering himself to settle between her thighs. His large erection pressed against her.

Tara palmed his cheek and kissed him. As her tongue played over his, she reached for him and guided him inside her body. A long, pleasurable groan rumbled inside Darren's chest.

Pulling his lips from hers, Darren looked down at her. There were no words in that moment. He entered her slowly, filling her completely, all the while still staring into her eyes. Tara couldn't be sure what was more pleasurable right then, the feeling of him inside her, or the feeling of intimacy that came from how their gazes locked at their first-ever moment of joining.

He pulled back, thrust deep. Pulled back, thrust deep. Releasing a moan, Tara wrapped her legs around him as their pace grew faster and faster.

She nipped at his neck, his slick flesh tasting of a hint of salt. She dug her nails into his back, her breath coming in quicker gasps as he continued to love her. She was nearing the point of climax.

Darren must have sensed that, because his strokes became faster and deeper, taking her body closer and closer to the edge.

And then Tara arched her neck as she cried out, her release as intense as it was glorious.

"Oh, Darren. Oh, baby . . ."

He didn't slow down, and as Tara's body was once again rocked with sweet spasms, Darren's body tensed with his own release. He held her tight, moaning loudly as he succumbed to his own climax.

The sound of their heavy breathing filled the air for several seconds. Neither moved.

Finally, Darren slid off Tara. Their bodies were slick with sweat, and the scent of their lovemaking filled the air.

"Oh, Darren." Tara sighed. "That was . . . amazing."

"I aim to please," Darren joked.

Tara giggled. "You're silly."

He wrapped his arm around her, and she snuggled against him. "Honestly," he whispered. "I agree with you. It was amazing."

Silence fell between them, and Tara savored the feeling of comfort that came from being in his arms. She had to admit, this felt good. Right.

She wanted to make love to him again.

Tara ran a finger down his belly, then lower.

Darren said, "What are you doing?"

"Nothing." Her hand covered him.

"That doesn't feel like nothing."

"No?"

Darren eased up, resting on an elbow. "No."

"Okay. Maybe I'm trying to seduce you . . ."

"Again?"

Tara smiled. "Again."

"You're doing a helluva job."

"Am I?"

"Uh-huh."

And then he covered her body again, kissing her softly and slowly, until the heat of passion engulfed them once more.

Sixteen

"David, did you hear back from the consolidators to see if we can offer my client the all-inclusive package at the price she wants?"

Tara stood at the edge of the cubicle to David's office, peering inside. He was the one who regularly called consolidators to see what packages were out there so that Wholesale Travel could get the best price for its clients.

"In fact, I just heard back from SunTime Vacations. Yep, they can get the price you want."

"Excellent."

Tara whirled around on her heel, a pep in her step. En route back to her desk, she halted when she saw Sharnette eyeing her with a suspicious look.

"What?" Tara asked, knowing she should probably continue on without saying a word.

"Someone seems particularly upbeat today." Sharnette raised a curious eyebrow. "I don't know . . . I'm thinking maybe she got lucky last night?"

"Shut up!" But Tara couldn't even say it with the conviction required to make her outrage seem believable.

"My goodness." Sharnette pushed her chair back and stood. "You did get lucky!"

A smile as wide as Texas spreading on her face, Tara approached Sharnette's desk. There was no point denying what was so obvious.

"Yes," she said in a hushed tone. "I did. And, girl, you were right. It was exactly what I needed. Why did I wait so long?"

Sharnette reached for Tara's hand and squeezed it while she squealed. "You have to tell me everything."

Tara shook her head. "No, I don't. I don't kiss and tell."

"At least tell me if it was Darren."

"Of course it was Darren!" Tara sighed happily. "And it was wonderful."

"It's about time."

Tara chuckled. "I guess so."

"Thinking about Harris at all?"

"Harris?" Tara scoffed. "Not a chance."

A satisfied grin tugged at Sharnette's lips. "That's my girl. Didn't I tell you that you needed a palette cleanser?"

"You did," Tara replied in a singsong voice. Her mind drifted to last night, and how incredible it had been making love with Darren. But dreaming about him all day would keep her from getting work done. "Listen, Sharnette, I've got to make some calls pronto."

"Go on. I can't even see my desk, there are so many envelopes I need to get out."

Tara went back to her desk and got back to work. After finalizing a couple of package deals to the Caribbean and one regularly scheduled airline ticket purchase, she sat back and stretched in her chair.

But her repose was short-lived. The phone rang again, and the light indicated it was a transfer to her extension. "Wholesale Travel. Tara speaking."

"Tara."

Tara froze at the sound of the voice.

"Tara?"

No, it couldn't be. She swallowed against the lump that had suddenly formed in her throat. "Harris?"

"Yes."

Oh, God. Why was he calling her now?

"I know, you're probably surprised that I'm calling you."

After a moment, Tara replied, "That's an understatement."

"I know, I should have called before. I meant to, but . . . I don't know."

Tara leaned forward, resting her elbows on the desk. She hated the way her stomach had tightened into a ball of knots. In a hushed tone, she asked, "How's your fiancée?"

A beat. "I . . . That's a fair question."

"Oh, is it now?"

"Yes. Listen, I know you have a lot of questions, and I want to answer them. . . . There are a lot of things we need to discuss, but I don't want to do it over the phone. Will you meet me for dinner, Tara? Give us a chance to talk?"

Was she in the twilight zone? This couldn't be real. Harris couldn't be on her phone line, much less asking her what it sounded like he was asking.

When Tara still didn't respond, Harris said, "Tara, please. We need to talk."

"*Talk?* Excuse me, Harris. But it's a little late for talk. You should have *talked* to me when you decided that you no longer wanted a relationship with me. You shouldn't have let me read about your engagement in the society pages of the paper." Pause. "By the way, I hope the boss's daughter makes you happy."

"Tara—"

She quickly disconnected the call. She was surprised to find her chest rising and falling quickly from harried breaths.

Her line rang again. She answered on the third ring. "Wholesale Travel, Tara speaking."

"Tara, don't hang up."

Tara immediately disconnected the call.

She stared at the phone, expecting it to ring. When it didn't, Tara's shoulders drooped in relief.

Good Lord, what did Harris want? Why was he calling now, so long after the fact?

Tara sat up and reached for the next folder, determined to put Harris out of her mind. She didn't care what he wanted.

As far as she was concerned, Harris could disappear off the face of the planet and it wouldn't bother her a bit.

"Hey, sexy," Tara said, much later that day. "I was just thinking about you."

"Only now? I've been thinking about you all day."

"Believe me, I haven't been able to stop thinking about you. Nor about what we shared last night." Tara paused, then added in a whisper, "I want more."

"Do you now?"

"Yes—and I'm wondering if you have any time tonight."

"Well, give me a second to check my schedule. Oh, guess what? You're in luck. Let me pencil you in."

"Hey, if it's too much trouble . . ."

"Not a chance."

Tara could hear the smile in Darren's voice, and it made her warm and tingly inside. "I can't wait to see you."

"Believe me, I've been dreaming of this all day. There's a possibility I may get called out for something tonight, but considering I've already been to three residences today to assess flood damage, I think my day's work is done. Which leaves me the entire evening free."

"You mean I can have you all night long?"

"Mmm . . . I love when you talk like that."

The memory of Harris's call entered Tara's mind, but she quickly blocked it. She didn't want to think of Harris, or what he wanted to say.

"Tara?"

"Huh?"

"I asked, when will you be finished with work?"

"Oh. I should be out of here in another hour. Then I have to fight the traffic back to Kendall."

"You gonna come straight here?"

"I figured I'd go home first." To freshen up.

"Naw. Just come here. I have a surprise for you."

That piqued Tara's interest. "You do?"

"Yeah."

"What is it?"

"You're not used to getting surprises, are you?"

Tara thought of Harris, how he'd surprised her with something special maybe three times in the five years they'd spent together. "No."

"Well, as long as you're dealing with me, get used to them."

"You don't play fair," Tara whined playfully.

"See—your curiosity is going to get the better of you, so you'll have to come over here as soon as possible."

"All right. I'll see you as soon as I can."

As Tara sat through rush-hour traffic, she couldn't stop wondering about what Darren's surprise might be.

With Darren, it could be anything. The man was as romantic as they came.

As much as Tara's curiosity was killing her, she knew she had to head home first. She wanted to change. The practical business suit she was wearing was appropriate for the office, but not for a rendezvous with one of the world's most romantic men.

The more she thought about it, the more Tara realized that her closet probably didn't have anything appropriate. She liked her clothes, but for tonight, she wanted something sexier.

Something that would turn Darren on the moment he saw her.

Yes, Tara decided, she was going to have to go shopping.

She needed something extra special for what she knew would be an extra-special night.

Seventeen

It was perfect.

Tara stepped back from her bathroom mirror to get a better view of her outfit.

The white summer dress had an innocent, yet sexy quality. Low cut, the dress was form-fitting on the top and accentuated her breasts, but it flared out at the hips and reached to above her knees. Tara had picked up a pair of white sling-back sandals to complete the sexy look.

Not to mention the lacy white push-up bra and matching thong she'd purchased at Victoria's Secret to wear beneath the dress.

Freshly showered, and her body creamed with a scented lotion, her makeup and hair completed, she was ready.

And she looked beautiful.

A smile touched her lips. She really was. She'd known she was attractive, but until Darren had told her she was beautiful—and meant it—she hadn't considered herself that.

Not counting the pimple that had sprung up on her chin, her skin was flawless. Her brown eyes were bright. What had Darren said? Mesmerizing. Maybe they were, she thought, smiling as she noticed a spark in her eyes she'd never seen before.

She wore simple makeup: mascara and a plum lipstick, but nothing else. She didn't need it.

Her hair was simple but elegant. She'd curled the ends, so they hung softly around her shoulders.

Again, her eyes perused her outfit in the mirror. She felt a little out of her element. This was the kind of outfit one wore for one reason only. Maybe she had gone overboard, but she wanted to look great. Better than great. She wanted Darren's mouth to fall open when he saw her.

Her heart fluttered with excitement at the thought of what he would think and feel when he saw her.

She should go, head to his place now that she was ready. Instead, Tara blew out a shaky breath.

She'd already spent the night with him, had had the best sex of her life with him, so why was she so nervous about seeing him this evening?

She didn't know.

Her palms literally sweat as she pressed them against the bathroom counter, leaning forward to stare at her reflection. She felt different about tonight, she realized. Yesterday had been about quenching her thirst with a man she was very attracted to. Tonight, if they ended up in bed again—and she had no doubt that they would—then she couldn't help but feel they would be taking their relationship to another level. Taking a step in the direction of a real relationship.

That had to be the cause for her nervousness.

Harris . . .

His name sounded in her mind so clearly, it

caused her stomach to churn. Lord help her, why was she thinking of him now?

Because of the message he'd left on her home phone.

"Tara, you can't ignore me forever. You know as well as I do that we need to talk."

Tara tried to inhale slow, steady breaths, but couldn't. Not with her heart going at probably a million beats a minute.

Closing her eyes tightly, she tried to force the memory of Harris's calls away.

She didn't need any complications in her life, not now. Harris was a complication.

Forcing her thoughts back to Darren, Tara wondered what his surprise was.

Well, there was only one way to find out.

Turning, Tara went into her bedroom, grabbed her purse, then headed out of her apartment.

If Darren's mouth fell open, Tara didn't notice. Her own mouth was slackened in surprise and wonder as she took in the sight before her.

A piece of magic had touched his house. Surely it had, for it wasn't the same place she'd seen just last week, but one that resembled something from a fairy tale.

The house was bathed in soft candlelight that danced against the walls in a seductive rhythm. The sweet scent of roses filled the air, making her head light. Or maybe it was the beguiling voice of Luther Vandross floating over the room that made her light-headed.

But as she felt his presence behind her, she knew it wasn't the music, or the flowers, or even the candles that made her light-headed. It was him. Only him. The one who'd created this fantasy.

"Is this real?" Tara didn't realize how breathless she was until she spoke.

"It's real." Darren's own voice was low and sexy, and as he spoke behind her, his voice vibrated through her body. She shut her eyes as the aftershocks of his voice rocked through her.

"My goodness, Darren. When you say surprise, you're definitely not joking."

"Come on," he said, placing his hands on her shoulders. Gently, he guided her through the open French doors and into the living room.

But when Tara stepped into the room, she jerked to a stop. For a moment, she couldn't speak. Couldn't breathe. The scene before her was so incredibly magical that it stole her voice and her breath. The furniture in the room had been moved and in its place lay a large, cream-colored comforter. Red rose petals were scattered over the blanket and large candles sat on each corner. In the center sat a white wicker basket, from which she could see the top of a wine bottle.

"When . . . how?"

"It wasn't hard. I started working on it after I talked to you. I wanted to do something really nice."

"I don't . . ." Her voice trailed off as a tear fell. She raised a hand to wipe it, but before she could, Darren stepped in front of her and framed her face with both hands. Gently, he used the pad of his thumb to brush away the tear.

"What's the matter?"

Her throat was so clogged with emotion that she couldn't speak.

He trailed his thumbs along her jaw. "Don't you like it?"

She wasn't sure if he was serious or teasing, but she wanted him to know that she loved it. So she tried to find a voice to express her feelings. "Oh, Darren . . ."

He smiled, and she relaxed. A simple smile could do that to her. His smile.

"What, sweetheart?"

Sweetheart. Nervous, she suddenly giggled. Then another tear fell. "Nobody has ever done anything like this for me."

"I'm glad," he said softly. "I'm glad that I'm the first."

"Why?" The question floated off a shaky breath.

"Hmm?"

"Are you this way with everyone, or just me? No, don't answer that."

"I'll answer that. I've always been a romantic, but no, I've never done anything like this for anyone before. I haven't had the desire—until you."

Was Darren truly for real? Or was someone going to pull the rug out from underneath her? Tara didn't want to get used to this, didn't want to fall for him, if it wasn't going to last.

The way it hadn't lasted with Harris.

Forget Harris.

Darren led her onto the blanket and urged her to sit. She did, extending her legs before her and crossing one sandal-clad foot over the other. He sat beside her, resting his arm across one knee.

The surprise wearing off, Tara asked, "What's in the basket?"

Darren gave her a charming smile, then reached for the wine. "White Zinfandel." He withdrew two wineglasses. "Fresh grapes." He lifted the green grapes for her inspection. "Fresh strawberries." He produced a bowl of strawberries, then lowered it onto the blanket. "And chocolate, of course." Winking, he lifted a silver bowl and passed it under her nose. The chocolate was melted for dipping. "I hear chocolate is the way to a woman's heart."

"You did all this for me?"

"No, I did it for the first person who was going to knock on my door today. That happened to be you."

Tara chuckled. "You're too much."

"Hopefully in a good way."

"Pinch me," Tara whispered, saying aloud what was in her heart. "I want to know this isn't a dream."

"How about I kiss you instead?"

She leaned forward to meet his face, but instead he took her hand and brought it to his mouth. Then he planted his thick lips over one knuckle and suckled softly.

Tell him, she told herself. *Tell him you want him right now.*

Releasing her hand, he reached for a large, ripe strawberry and dipped it in the chocolate. His eyes holding hers, he brought the strawberry to her mouth. When she opened her mouth to receive it, he pulled it back.

"Tell me how much you want it," he said.

"Oh, I want it."

He brought it to her lips, but instead of letting her eat it, he ran the tip of the strawberry over her lips, leaving chocolate covering her mouth. "Sorry," he said. "Let me get that."

Leaning into her, he flicked his tongue slowly

over her lips, licking off the chocolate. Lord help her, this was too erotic. Her core pulsed as she imagined his tongue in a very different region, bringing her to the edge of oblivion.

As his tongue played over her mouth, she flicked her own tongue out to meet his. The tips met, danced. Then she reached for the strawberry, but their hands collided and the chocolate-covered fruit fell—right onto her bosom, then onto her white dress.

But she didn't even care.

Pulling back, Darren glanced down. "Damn, your dress."

"It's okay—"

"You sure? I think you should take it off."

She raised an eyebrow as she understood his meaning. "Do you now?"

"Well, it is soiled." He ran a finger over the spot on her breast where the chocolate had stained the dress. Then he dipped his head and licked the chocolate off her cleavage.

Tara moaned softly, running a hand over his head softly. "You're right," she managed between ragged breaths. "I should get out of this. Will you, uh . . . I can't reach the zipper."

"My pleasure."

But before he ventured to the zipper, he slipped his hands beneath one thin strap, pulled it down, then planted a kiss on her shoulder. He kept his lips on her body, moving them to her back, kissing her spine as he unzipped the dress.

She purred.

"Do you want me, Tara?"

"You know I do," she replied in a hoarse voice as his lips reached the bottom of her back.

"Then show me," he said, moving to face her. "Show me how much."

Suddenly nervous, she asked, "What do you want me to do?"

He lay back on the blanket. "Whatever you want."

Tara swallowed. She didn't know what to do, if she'd turn him on the way he was able to turn her on. But as he stared up at her from narrowed eyes, she realized he wasn't concerned. He trusted her.

And he wanted her.

She let her eyes wander over his face, then lower to the white T-shirt he wore, lower to his jeans. She could see his arousal, large and hard, beneath the denim. So, leaning forward to sit on her knees, she reached for him and stroked him.

And felt a surge of power as he moaned.

She stroked him again, felt him pulsate against her hand. She ran her hand upward to his firm stomach, where she splayed her fingers, enjoying the feel of the muscles beneath. She pushed his shirt up and brought her other hand to his chest. She stroked a nipple with her fingers.

Then with her tongue.

Closing his eyes, he blew out a ragged breath.

Feeling incredibly sexy, Tara pulled up her skirt to her hips and straddled him. Then, leaning forward, she allowed her dress to fall from her body, exposing her bra. As she brought her lips down onto his flat nipple again, she heard a deep rumbling within his chest. Felt it.

He took her by the shoulders and eased her forward, until her breasts hung over his face. Urgently, he dragged the bra down over one nipple, then hungrily took it into his mouth. He suckled hard. Tara cried out from the pleasure of it, then cried out again as he pleasured the other nipple with equal fervor.

She thought she would die right there.

Somehow she found the strength not to collapse and pulled back from him. And somehow she found the strength to be more bold than she had ever been in her life. She reached for his hand and brought it to the apex of her thighs, forcing him to feel the wet spot. "That's how much I want you."

She reached for the snap of his jeans, but he took her wrists in one hand and whirled her over so that she was on her back. Her shoe hit a bowl as he moved her, and they both looked to see what had spilled. The strawberries.

Darren gave her a soft but sensual kiss on the lips. "Wait here."

As if she'd go anywhere!

He loaded the wine, glasses, strawberries, and grapes into the wicker basket, then moved the basket to the floor. He did the same with the candles, and as he looked at her and smiled, he said, "Fire hazard."

The only fire hazard was him, and he'd already ignited her body so completely that there was no way her fire could be doused.

As she lay on her back, her dress pulled down below her breasts, he returned to her side. He held the silver bowl. The chocolate.

Oh, God. He wasn't going to—

He did. Using a finger, he dipped it into the chocolate, then smothered the dark cream onto both her nipples. He took his time—and his pleasure—licking off the chocolate as she moaned and writhed beneath him.

Darren had never done anything like this before,

and before tonight, he hadn't even thought of it. But Tara brought out a wild side in him he didn't even know existed.

"Tell me, Tara. Did you wear this because you knew it would turn me on?"

"I hoped. I . . ." She moaned when Darren took a nipple in his mouth.

"Hmm?"

"I bought the entire outfit today."

Darren groaned as he took her nipple fully into his mouth, suckling as hard as he could. Tara gripped his head, her own head tossing from side to side.

God, he couldn't get enough of her. Maybe it was the white dress, his favorite color on a woman. Or maybe it was the reality that she was so eager for him that her body quivered beneath his every touch.

He didn't know, and right now he didn't care. He only wanted to feel, to taste, to enjoy.

Reaching beneath her dress, he found her white panties and forced a finger beneath them. She was wet for him. Ready. He took the condom from his jeans pocket and rolled it on.

He was going to pull her underwear off, but he remembered the shoes, and he liked the shoes, so he simply spread her legs and positioned himself between them, nudging the underwear to the side to allow him access. Then he thrust into her with one hard movement.

She cried out, music to his ears, urging him on. But it wasn't like he needed any encouragement. He wanted her with a need unlike anything he'd ever known.

He thrust harder, deeper. She wrapped her legs around his hips and squeezed—and he nearly lost it. So he slowed his pace, for he didn't want to disappoint her.

Together they found a new rhythm, slower, still seductive, their bodies dancing in the candlelight to the soft sounds of Luther Vandross. But he could barely hear the music when all he cared about were the mewling sounds escaping her lips.

Slipping a hand between their bodies, he massaged her, and the next second, she dug her nails into his back and cried out with her release. And then he couldn't hold back any longer. He fell over the edge, shattering into a million pieces as he landed.

And as he lay on top of her, his mouth over hers, their ragged breaths mingling, Darren wondered if he hadn't just found a piece of heaven.

God, Darren loved her.

It was the middle of the night, and after making love many more times, they were now in his bed, recuperating.

But Darren couldn't sleep. All he could do was look at her.

He loved everything about her, physically and otherwise. Her breasts, visible because the sheets only covered her to her midriff, were firm and enticing. Reaching for them, he let his hands hover over them, pretending they were actually touching her flesh. Then he brought his hand back to his side and let his eyes roam from her breasts and up the expanse of her honey-colored neck, then upward to her face. Her full lips were slightly parted as though she were inviting him to kiss her. Even in sleep, she was seductive.

Darren slipped an arm around her waist and gently rested his head against hers.

Tonight felt like a step in a new direction.

Tonight, it felt as if they'd officially become boyfriend and girlfriend.

Eighteen

A scream erupted from Diamond's throat when she opened her car door and saw the bouquet of roses on her front seat.

Well, what *had* been a bouquet of roses.

There were red rose petals everywhere. Someone had clearly smashed the bouquet until almost every petal had fallen off.

Anger. That's what this indicated.

Lord help her, someone had gotten into her car. She whirled around, but saw nothing out of the ordinary in the station's parking lot.

But she wasn't safe. Someone wanted to hurt her.

She turned and ran back to the building.

The decision at the station had been easy. Ken Potter, the station manager, had told Diamond to take the rest of the day off. They would run a repeat of one of her shows for the night broadcast.

Diamond had called Paul, but he was working the evening shift this week and she hadn't been able to reach him. Then, she'd called Tara, but Tara wasn't home.

On her way out of the station, both Ken and Rick

had urged her to go to the police. They didn't have to say it; they were gravely concerned.

Her stomach fluttering with nerves, Diamond drove to the North Miami Police Department she'd been to before with Tara. Once inside, she asked for Detective Perez.

"Have a seat," the receptionist told her. "I'll let him know you're here."

What seemed like hours later, Detective Perez appeared. His eyes registered concern the moment he saw Diamond.

Diamond stood and hurried to him. Seeing him made her realize just how scared she was. If this was another Clay situation, she had no clue how she was going to deal with it. She was coming undone, unraveling at the seams.

In Detective Perez's office, Diamond began to speak before she sat down. "He got into my car. My *car.* I'm not safe. Not anywhere."

"Have a seat. And start over."

Diamond did as he said, telling her story from the beginning. She told him about the roses, how someone had gotten into her car easily. There was no sign of forcible entry.

"Any note this time?" Detective Perez asked.

Diamond shook her head. "No. Just the smashed roses. And that scares me. It was a warning. I know it. But from who? I mean, how can this person know so much about me? Like my cousin's phone number. Where she works. What kind of car I drive."

Detective Perez studied Diamond. After a moment, he asked, "Is there anyone you know who might want to hurt you?"

"No."

"Most people can't imagine anyone wanting to

hurt them, especially not people they know. I know it's not a pleasant thought to contemplate, but it's something you have to consider. Yes, I understand that you're a celebrity, and as such you are at risk of having strangers harass and stalk you. But the culprit could also be someone close to you."

"I highly doubt that," Diamond said quickly.

"Believe me, I know you don't want to consider it. But based on the facts—based on your own questions—that would be my guess. That the person doing this is someone close to you. Think about it: of your family, friends, and colleagues, is there anyone you can imagine trying to hurt you?"

"I don't know. It could be a colleague, I guess." But who? Rick? Someone she had only a passing acquaintance with? "I'll have to think about it."

And that's where she left things with Detective Perez. He made a note of the latest incident, but instructed her long and hard to think about who she knew that might possibly want to hurt her.

She didn't want to believe that he might be on the right track. But as Diamond drove home, she couldn't help wondering if Detective Perez was right.

Did she know the person who wanted to hurt her?

Tara was awakened by the sound of talking. Rolling over, she realized that she was not in her own bed. A smile formed on her lips as she remembered the absolutely incredible evening she had spent with Darren.

Where was he?

She could hear him speaking, she realized, but

he wasn't in the room. Sitting up, she strained to hear where he was.

". . . later. Yes, I'm going to do my best. I can't make any promises. . . . Tomorrow."

Darren must have been on the phone. Rising, Tara wrapped the blanket around her body and headed out to the living room.

"Darren?" she called softly.

When she reached the entrance of the living room, Darren's back was to her as he sat on the edge of his sofa. Again she called his name.

Darren whirled around, his eyes registering surprise as he looked at her. He quickly said into the receiver, "I have to go." Then he hung up.

Strolling toward him, Tara looked at him curiously. "You're up early. Who was that?"

"No one."

"That didn't sound like no one." Tara smiled to say she wasn't pressuring him, but that she hoped he'd tell her. Darren bit his lip. "It was work."

"Is everything okay?"

"Yeah, yeah. Everything's fine."

"Are you sure?"

"Of course I'm sure."

His tone did not match his words. After sharing such a passionate night with him, Tara felt the sting that came from rejection. But she wasn't going to press the issue. Whatever was going on was none of her business.

"I was lonely," Tara said. She stepped toward him. "Cold. I could use a little warming up."

One arm holding the blanket to her chest, she put the other around Darren's neck and raised herself on her toes until her lips met his. But he did not kiss her back the way she had hoped.

"Darren, something *is* wrong."

"I've just got a lot on my mind. And I've got to get ready now for work. Early meeting."

"Oh." Tara couldn't hide her disappointment.

"I'm sorry."

"Don't worry about it," Tara said. But her stomach dropped to her knees. Something didn't feel right. "I—I have to go home, get a shower, head to work."

She started for the bedroom. Darren fell into step beside her. "Tara," he began, "you don't have to rush off."

"No, I do." *Our magical night is over. Back to reality . . .*

Tara walked into the bedroom. She immediately went to the chair where she'd placed her clothes. When she reached for them, Darren took hold of her arm. Turning, she faced him.

"I love you, Tara."

The words made her heart flutter, even though he'd already told her this once before. "Then why don't you tell me what's going on? Why are you suddenly pushing me away?"

"I'm not pushing you away."

"It seems like it to me."

He stroked her chin. "It's not you. Like I said, I have a lot on my mind. Work. There are some things going on that need my attention."

Then he kissed her, sweetly, and Tara felt some of her apprehension ebb away.

"I still have a bit of time," Darren whispered in her ear. "If you want to get a shower with me . . ."

Tara smiled. "I thought you'd never ask."

* * *

"If Harris calls again, do *not* put him through. I have no desire to talk to him."

Sharnette nodded, then asked, "What's going on?"

"Hell if I know. But I don't want to know. I am finally putting Harris behind me once and for all."

Tara turned and headed to her desk. She knew she was leaving Sharnette with a ton of questions, but there was no point talking about the situation because she didn't have any answers.

By the end of the day, Harris had called three times. Sharnette had taken his messages and passed them on to Tara, because Harris had insisted.

Tara had the craziest feeling that Harris was going to show up at her office, so when the news broadcast that there was a tropical storm coming, Tara decided to call it a day. She had to head back to Kendall, and U.S.-1 was prone to flooding in certain areas.

But as she said her good-byes and made her way to the door, the door chimes sang. Tara's head whipped up, her heart pounding with fear. A smile erupted on her face when she saw Darren.

"Hey, you." Tara was relieved to see him, considering she'd expected she might see Harris. She hurried toward Darren and gave him a brief hug.

"Hey, beautiful."

"What are you doing here?"

"I wanted to see you. Looks like I just caught you."

"Yeah. I was on my way out. The weather." *Harris . . .*

"Going home?"

"Mmm-hmm."

"Want any company?"

The sound of a clearing throat got Tara's attention, and she spun around. Sharnette smiled sweetly at her.

"Oh. Where are my manners? Darren, this is Sharnette. Sharnette, Darren."

Darren and Sharnette shook hands.

Janice was suddenly beside them, offering her hand to Darren.

"And this is Janice," Tara said. "They are both two of my very good friends."

"We've heard wonderful things about you," Janice said, beaming.

"That's good to hear." Darren glanced at Tara. "Actually, I'd been hoping to combine business with pleasure."

"Oh?"

"I was wondering if we could go over some cruise packages."

Tara nodded. "Of course." She had wanted to leave, but she could spend a few minutes to take care of this for Darren. "Let's go to my desk."

Once there, Tara selected the various cruise brochures. "Now—"

"I figured I'd let you choose the destination," Darren announced before she could continue.

Tara gaped at him. "What did you say?"

"I trust you. I'm sure whatever you choose will be fine."

Tara drew in a slow breath, a mixture of amazement and surprise filling her. "You're sure?"

"Yes. All you'll need from me are the dates, and the money." He smiled.

"In that case." Tara considered the options, then said, "Caribbean. You say your family is Jamaican. I'm sure they love the place where they grew up, but if they're like most people, they haven't traveled all over the world. Have they been to other islands?"

"No, actually."

"Then I can book them on a Caribbean cruise so that they can see other islands, as well as the one where they grew up."

"See—that's why I trusted this to you."

Tara couldn't help feeling a moment of pride. It wasn't that she'd done anything extraordinary; she'd made suggestions that many of her customers had loved. But knowing that she had truly pleased Darren left her feeling extra pleased.

"What are the dates?"

"The first week in November. Saturday to Saturday."

Tara jotted down the information. "You want to take care of all this now? Payment and all?"

"May as well."

Tara researched the trip, found the best ship and accommodations for the best price, then confirmed the reservation with Darren's credit card. Once finished with everything, she announced, "That's it. Easy as pie. Sharnette will send the tickets out as soon as they come in. Do you want them to go to you?"

"Yes. This is a surprise."

Tara made some more notes, then left the file on her desk so she could deal with the small details in the morning. When she stood, Darren did too.

"You ready?" Darren asked.

"Yep."

"Bye, guys." Tara waved to everyone in the office, then playfully stuck her tongue out at Sharnette when she saw her giving Darren's body a slow perusal while biting on a finger. Sharnette giggled.

"Let's get out of here," Tara told Darren, taking his arm and leading him to the door.

Once outside the office, Tara said, "You want to follow me to my place?"

"Sure."

The rain didn't let up as they drove. In fact, it got worse. The winds wreaked havoc with the palm trees along U.S.-1. At one of the intersections, the traffic lights had gone haywire, causing chaos as traffic tried to drive through the intersection.

Tara was relieved when she made it to her apartment complex without incident. She parked as close to her apartment as she could get, and Darren pulled into the spot next to her.

Tara exited her car when she saw Darren open his door. "Quick," she yelled, chuckling as she ran to her apartment door. She opened it and rushed inside. Darren was fast on her heels, but when she turned she saw that he, like her, hadn't been able to escape getting drenched. Seeing the newspaper he'd used as a makeshift umbrella, Tara burst into laughter.

"Oh, you think this is funny, do you?"

"Like that newspaper was going to do anything for you."

Darren gave a nonchalant shrug. "Well, a guy's got to try. I'm glad I could at least provide you with some entertainment."

"You always make me laugh."

"In a good way, I hope."

Tara's breathing quickened as Darren slowly closed the distance between them. "Yes. . . ."

"You are . . ." His voice trailed off, as though he had been robbed of his breath. "So beautiful. Especially when you're wet."

Tara's body warmed at the sexual meaning behind Darren's words, even though she was sure he didn't intend it. The reaction startled her.

"Um . . . I think I should change." Tara forced a laugh to try and ease the sexual tension that was suddenly so thick, you could cut it. "You too. To get out of these wet clothes, I mean. I'll get you a shirt. Or maybe I won't."

She whirled around quickly, but Darren caught her by the wrist, stopping her. Her heart did a jiggy in her chest as she slowly turned to face him.

Never had one of Harris's looks made her entire body flush the way Darren's did. Was it normal to want someone as much sexually as she wanted Darren?

"I'm beginning to wonder if you want me just for my body."

Tara threw her head back and laughed.

"That's funny, is it?"

"Of course it's funny."

"Are you going to deny that you want to get me naked now so you can have your wicked way with me?"

"Darren!"

"Come on. Deny it."

Tara shook her head as she stared at him. "So, if I want to make love to you, what does that mean?"

"I think we should see how long we can actually last without sex."

Tara giggled. "Why?"

"Because . . ." Darren lowered his head and nibbled on her ear. "I want to make sure you want me for more than my body."

"Oh, and that's supposed to be easy with you nibbling on my ear . . ." Tara mewled, wrapping her arms around Darren's neck.

"Forget what I said. I'd only be torturing myself if we didn't make love."

A feeling of power washed over Tara as she realized she was as irresistible to Darren as he was to her.

"Let's get out of these clothes," Tara said. "After all, they're wet."

"I like you wet," Darren said, his voice as thick and rich as melted chocolate.

And then his other hand was on her face, his fingers gently skimming her skin. Tara's eyelids fluttered shut as her knees literally weakened.

She'd never thought it possible that first day she'd met him, but Darren had wormed his way into her heart with his old-fashioned values and gentleman qualities.

And his ability to romance her in a way she'd never before been romanced.

Suddenly, she wanted him to take her in his arms and kiss her silly.

As if in answer to her unspoken thoughts, Darren swept her into his arms and covered her lips with his, all in one thrilling moment. Tara sighed into his mouth, her body melting in his arms. Her hands crept around his neck and her fingertips flirted with the skin at his nape.

A passionate sound rumbled in Darren's chest. Tara felt it first, and then the sound left his mouth and went into hers. God, she wanted him. He had unleashed the sexual monster in her, and she was loving every minute of it.

Tara opened her mouth, allowing Darren's tongue to delve inside. She arched into him, flattening her soft breasts against his hard chest. Woman to man. The way it was supposed to be.

"I'm falling for you, Darren Burkeen."

Darren pulled away and looked down at her, a look that wondered at the meaning of her words.

Tara met the look dead-on, her gaze never wavering, then slipped her arms around his neck and kissed him again, hoping her actions would show him all he needed to know.

Darren kissed her back, his lips moving slowly yet enticingly over hers. But like a pot slowly simmering to a boil, the kiss grew hotter, more urgent. And suddenly, Darren's hands were over her face, then in her hair, pulling her closer.

The sudden pounding on the door was like a douse of cold water. Darren stepped away from her and gave her a curious look.

"Who could that be?" Tara wondered aloud. She didn't expect Diamond. Not that it would be the first time her cousin had shown up unannounced.

When the knocking persisted, Tara said, "Give me a moment. That's probably my cousin, Diamond. I'll get rid of her." Then she did her best at a seductive smile. "I definitely want to pick up where we left off. So don't you even think of taking off through a window."

"You couldn't get rid of me now if you tried."

A smile touched Tara's lips, and she stared at him, wanting nothing more than to kiss him again and lose herself in the essence of this man.

There was another knock. "I better get that."

"Go ahead."

Darren lingered behind her while Tara headed to the door. She turned the knob and swung it open, the words "Diamond, your timing sucks" ready to form on her lips.

But when she saw who was at the door, the words lodged in her throat. The girlish smile on her lips instantly disappeared.

Lord have mercy. It wasn't Diamond.

"Hello, Tara." A confident smile played on his lips. "Aren't you going to invite me in?"

Nineteen

"Harris." Tara finally found her voice.

"You left me no choice," he said. "You wouldn't take my calls, you didn't agree to see me. I called your office, and Sharnette said you'd left for the day. That's why I came over."

Tara kept the door closed as much as she could, blocking Harris from seeing inside her apartment. "Harris, you can't . . . you can't just show up here."

"All I want is a few minutes, Tara. A few minutes to explain why I've been such an idiot." He gave a bold perusal of her body, blowing out a swoosh of air as he did. "Tara, I have missed you."

When his eyes met hers again, Tara gave him a steely glare.

"Sorry. That was out of line. Tara, I was stupid. A complete moron for leaving you."

Regret actually shone in his eyes, and Tara could only look at him, completely baffled. Her eyes roamed the length of his body, from his designer shoes up to his designer suit, finally stopping when she reached his face. She took it all in, finding herself more appalled by his gall with each passing second. He didn't even look like the Harris she'd known. This one looked arrogant, like he was concerned with outward appearances more than any-thing else.

Which, Tara reflected sadly, was true. It was why he'd gotten engaged to his boss's daughter, she was sure.

When Harris stepped forward, as if trying to walk into her apartment, Tara's anger sprang forth. "You have no right to be here, Harris."

"I don't expect you not to be angry—"

"Angry? Angry doesn't even begin to describe what I'm feeling."

"Why are you whispering?" Harris asked.

"Because . . ." Tara blew out an aggravated breath. "Because I don't want to fight with you. I don't want the neighbors thinking there's a prob-lem."

"I don't want to fight, either. And if you don't want the neighbors thinking anything is wrong, then you should invite me in."

"No."

"Come on, Tara. Won't you at least let me ex-plain?"

"You need to leave." Tara started to close the door, but Harris put a hand on it, stopping her.

Tara glanced uneasily over her shoulder. Darren's eyes met hers. She saw confusion in their depths.

She turned back to Harris. "Good-bye."

Ignoring her, he pushed past her into her apart-ment.

Tara cringed. No, this couldn't be happening.

"Harris—"

"Who's this?" Harris asked, stopping short when he saw Darren. His voice was full of attitude, as if he still had a right to her.

When Tara didn't say anything, Darren spoke. "Maybe I should go."

Tara started for Darren. "No. I don't want you to leave."

"Is this Harris?" Darren asked.

"Yes, and he was just leaving."

"Not until I talk to you. We have unfinished business." Harris faced Darren. "Harris Seeman."

Harris extended his hand and Darren shook it. "Darren Burkeen."

There was a moment of silence; then Harris said, "You know my name, so I'm assuming you know who I am. I'd appreciate it if you'd give me some time alone with Tara."

Tara whirled to face Harris. "You—"

"All I want is a moment to talk to you," Harris explained, as though she were the one who was being unreasonable.

"No. This isn't right. You can't—you can't just—" Tara could hardly get the words out as Darren stepped past them, toward the door.

"Darren, don't go. Please wait—"

Harris said, "I appreciate this, Darren."

"And what about me?" Tara asked. "What about what's important to me?"

"Don't do this, Tara," Harris said softly. "Not after what we meant to each other."

Darren gave Harris a pointed look, then moved his gaze to Tara. "Tara, I don't know what's going on right now, but I don't want to be in the middle of it. Maybe you should talk to him."

"But—"

"No, I think there are some things he needs to hear from you. It's not my place."

This was the last moment Tara needed Darren to

be gentlemanly! But he stepped past her and quietly left. Tara felt empty watching him go.

She knew he was hurting. She'd seen it in his eyes. He had no clue what was going on with her and Harris.

If she still loved him.

When the door closed behind Darren, Tara turned to Harris. "Thanks a lot, you . . . you jerk."

Looking at her calmly, Harris said, "So, is he the reason you didn't return my calls? The reason you didn't want me here now?"

"Do you hear yourself? You're the one who got engaged to someone else, remember?"

"I want you back, Tara."

Harris's confession rendered her speechless.

"There is no explanation for what I did." Harris sighed. "Except to say I was a fool."

"You're *engaged.*"

"Not anymore. I couldn't go through with it. Aisha is Daddy's little girl, and when I really stopped to see what my life was going to be, I couldn't live with it." He stopped, stepped toward her. "Couldn't live without you."

When Harris's hand framed her face, Tara took a hasty step backward.

Harris blew out a ragged breath. "Okay. I understand. And you're right. I can't come back here and expect everything to be the way it was. But I still want you back in my life, and I'm prepared to do whatever it takes."

"You can't do this to me."

"You loved me for five years, Tara. Don't expect me to believe that you've stopped."

"You ended things."

"I was an idiot."

Tara's heart beat a mile a minute. "You have to go. You have to—"

"Because that's what you want, or because that's what you think is best?"

Tara turned away from him, hugging her torso. "I can't deal with you right now, Harris. You have to understand."

When she felt his hands on her shoulders, Tara's back went rigid.

"God, Tara. I'm so sorry I hurt you." His voice was tender, and that made Tara's heart crack. "I swear to you, I know now. I know how much I love you. I would never, ever hurt you again."

Tara didn't respond, and Harris's hands slipped off her shoulders. She heard the rustling of his clothes as he moved to the door.

When she heard the door open, Tara closed her eyes. Seeing Harris again shouldn't have unnerved her the way it had, but her insides were twisted in painful knots.

"Think about what I said, Tara. I still love you, and I'll do whatever it takes to get you back."

Then the door clicked shut.

Tara instantly spun around, making sure he was gone.

He was.

Frustration overwhelming her, Tara grabbed a pillow from her sofa and threw it at the door.

Then she sank onto her sofa, burying her face in her hands.

Clearly, Harris meant business. The next day, a dozen long-stemmed roses arrived at her workplace.

"My, my, my," Sharnette said, sniffing the scent

of the red roses. "Who would have thought?" She looked at Tara over the flowers. "Now, you've got two men vying for your attention. I tell you, you need to get new business cards printed up with the new name of the business—Wholesale Flowers and Gifts."

Sharnette's attempt at humor failed to make Tara smile.

After a moment, Sharnette spoke seriously. "So, what do you plan to do?"

For the gazillionth time that day, Tara sighed. She looked up at Sharnette and Janice with what she knew had to be the most melancholy expression possible.

"I don't know what I'm going to do," she replied honestly. And she didn't. She felt confused. And she felt bad for Darren. How must he have felt about Harris showing up at her door like that? She'd left Darren a couple of messages, hoping he'd call her back to talk about the situation, but he hadn't gotten back to her yet.

"Harris obviously wants you back," Janice said.

"But why?" Tara asked. "That's what I keep asking myself. I mean, he dumped me without even telling me first! Something must have happened with the boss's daughter."

"Maybe it did," Janice said.

"Or maybe he truly came to his senses."

Tara frowned. "It doesn't matter. . . ." But her words sounded weak even to her own ears.

"I know you like Darren," Sharnette began, "but I also know how hard it is to resist exes sometimes."

"He has no right," Tara complained.

"Maybe not," Sharnette replied. "But what does right have to do with matters of the heart?"

"I like Darren. I'm falling for him. This is the last thing I need."

Neither Janice nor Sharnette said anything, both of them looking at her with sympathetic expressions. Then, Sharnette spoke. "You still care for him. For Harris."

"N—" Tara stopped short. Blew out a sad breath. "I don't know."

Sharnette tsked. "Girl, you are in a bind."

"I'm not in love with him anymore. I don't want to be with him. But—"

"But it's hard to sweep five years of memories under the rug in little over a month," Janice finished for her.

Tara sighed sadly.

Sharnette rounded the desk and placed a hand on her shoulder. "I've been there. I know it's not easy. If you need me, I'm here."

"Me too," Janice added.

"Thanks."

Tara watched her two friends head back to their desks. She tried Darren once more, but again, he didn't answer the phone.

She was certain he was working, but in the past when she'd called his home number, he'd returned her call a short time later. Was he deliberately ignoring her now?

Tara groaned. She wished he would call her back. If he was insecure about her feelings for Harris, that was understandable, but he wasn't even giving her a chance to explain anything.

The more Tara sat and thought about the situation, the more she realized she'd blown it when Harris had come to the door. Harris had completely shocked her by showing up unannounced, and not wanting Darren to know who was there, she'd started whispering. But looking back, she saw now that it seemed she was trying to keep the truth from Darren. And it had backfired anyway, because Harris had had no plans to leave, despite her wishes.

Still, the last thing Darren should have done now was ignore her.

Tara stared at her phone, willing Darren to call. He didn't.

After half an hour passed, Tara said softly, "You know what, I don't care if he calls." That wasn't exactly true, but Tara knew she had to put Darren and Harris out of her mind for the time being. She had work to do. Work that wouldn't get done if she continued to worry about her personal life.

Still, as Tara slid her chair closer to her desk and surveyed the files, she couldn't help muttering with annoyance, "Men!"

Twenty

Tara's mouth fell open in shock when she went home and heard the message from Darren.

"Tara, hi. I want to let you know I've gotten your messages, but I'm at the airport right now. I'm heading out of town on a sudden business trip. I won't be back until at least tomorrow night. I'll give you a call then."

Tara replayed the message, listening for something she hadn't heard the first time. Of course, there was nothing else.

She sank onto her sofa, wondering what was really going on. Was Darren brushing her off? Just like that?

Her chest tightening with pain, Tara tried to pretend it didn't matter. She'd barely started seeing him, and if after all he'd told her, he was so quick to write her off, then she was better off without him.

But whether or not that was true, Tara didn't feel any better about the situation.

Diamond wanted to let the phone go unanswered when it rang shortly after ten that morning. She was tired, and not in the least bit interested in speaking to anyone.

But she was smart enough to know that she had to answer the phone. It could be work-related.

"Hello?"

"Hi, Diamond. It's Shelley from the office."

"Oh, hi, Shelley." Shelley worked in the apartment's leasing office.

"I just want to let you know that there's a package here for you."

"Really?" Normally, packages were delivered to one's apartment first, then left at the office if there was no one home.

"Yeah. Norm said he knocked and knocked, but no one answered."

Norm was the UPS deliveryman. "All right, I'll be there as soon as I can."

Diamond dressed quickly. Perhaps the radio station had sent her something. It wouldn't be the first time.

She retrieved the small brown box from the office, then returned to her apartment. The return address and name she did not recognize.

In the kitchen, Diamond used a knife to cut the tape and open the box. She opened it and looked inside.

A scream bubbled in her throat as she saw the contents of the box.

It was a picture of her taken at a recent mall function. But someone had cut out her eyes, and written the word *Whore* across her face.

But the words at the bottom of the picture were what scared her the most.

I'm going to kill you.

The scream finally escaped. Dropping the box to the floor, Diamond ran to her bedroom. She had to get out of there.

He knows where I live. He knows where I work. I'm not safe.

Oh, God.

Diamond called Paul's cell, but he didn't answer, which meant he was probably at a job. "Damn it, Paul. I need you now!"

She tried again, and again got no answer.

As she replaced the receiver, her head jerked up at a sound. Her heart slammed against her rib cage. What was *that?*

She waited only a moment longer before grabbing her keys from her night table. She wasn't going to stay around here and be a sitting duck for this creep who wanted to kill her.

She had to get out of here.

Diamond got in her car and drove, not knowing where she was going. What if someone was following her, right now?

She had to go to the police, she realized. But damn, she'd forgotten the box. She needed it.

After a quick glance around, Diamond pulled a U-turn.

Then screamed the moment before the SUV slammed into her.

Tara was on the phone with a client when Sharnette came up to her desk, frantically trying to get her attention.

"Um, can you hold, Jim?"

"Sure."

Tara placed Jim on hold, then looked up at Sharnette. "What is it?"

"There's an urgent call for you."

"Who is it?"

"I don't know. It's a man."

Tara's stomach lurched. "Darren?"

"I don't think so. But no, it wasn't Harris."

With Jim on hold, Tara pressed the flashing line. "Wholesale Travel, Tara speaking."

"Tara. Thank God. I've been trying to reach you for hours, but I didn't know which travel agency you worked at . . ."

"Paul?" Tara asked.

"Yeah, it's me."

Instantly, the hairs on Tara's nape stood on end. "What is it, Paul? What's wrong?"

"It's Diamond."

"God, no."

"She's been in an accident."

"No." Panic filled her. "Is she okay?"

"She's in the hospital."

Thank you, thank you. "Which one?"

"Jackson Memorial."

"I'm on my way."

The sight of her cousin lying with her eyes closed on the hospital bed made Tara's heart crack. Her head was wrapped in a bandage, and the right side of her face was swollen.

But, thank the Lord, she was alive.

Paul was dressed in his police uniform, indicating he'd come right from work and had been here ever since.

"Paul."

Hearing his name, Paul turned. A sad smile lifted his lips when he saw Tara. Rising from the chair beside the bed where he'd been holding Diamond's hand, he went to Tara and wrapped her in a hug.

"What happened?" Tara asked.

"I don't know. I got a call that she'd been in an accident. All I know is that she wasn't far from the apartment when it happened. I'm not sure where she was going."

"Who hit her?"

"Some guy in an SUV. He said she pulled a U-turn right in front of him. That doesn't seem like Diamond, but all the witnesses corroborate his story."

Tara couldn't help wondering what had happened. Diamond was a cautious driver. Had something caused her to be distracted? With the recent stalker harassing her, had something scared her?

None of that mattered now, Tara realized.

Paul's gaze went over his shoulder, back to Diamond. Tara followed his line of sight, moving closer to her cousin.

"Is she . . . is she unconscious?"

"Sedated. She was conscious when she was admitted, but in a lot of pain. The doctors say she'll be all right, but I figured you should know."

"Of course."

"And since Diamond's parents are out of town . . ."

"They're in New York, visiting family."

"So you can reach them?"

"Yes." Tara blew out a shaky breath. "Yes."

She walked to the bed and stared down at Diamond, her heart aching. Her cousin's beautiful face was bruised and swollen. The skin was broken on the right side of her mouth.

"Oh, Diamond." Tara reached for her hand. "What happened, Diamond?"

Paul stood beside her. "She looks bad, but the doctor assures me it's all superficial bruises and contusions. In fact, he says she can probably go home tomorrow."

Paul went back to the chair he'd been sitting in and resumed his position beside Diamond. Tara watched him watching her.

And suddenly thought of Darren. Where was he right now?

"Have you eaten anything?" Tara asked Paul.

"No."

"I'll grab you a sandwich and a soda."

"Thanks. That'd be great."

Tara stepped away from the bed, and Paul instantly took Diamond's hand in his. She continued to watch them a moment, then slipped quietly out of the room in search of the cafeteria.

Nearly three hours later, Diamond opened her eyes. She'd been tossing back and forth for a little while, whimpering softly. Tara had held her hand while Paul had stroked her forehead. Finally, with both of them at her side, she'd woken.

At first, Diamond looked around, clearly confused by her surroundings.

"There was an accident," Paul explained. "You're in the hospital."

Diamond made a movement that resembled a nod.

"It's okay," Paul said. "Take it easy. You're going to be fine."

Diamond closed her eyes, once again resting.

About half an hour later, she opened her eyes and suddenly said, "He knows where I live."

"Who, Diamond?" Tara asked.

"The guy who's been harassing me," Diamond answered slowly.

"Was he there?" Paul asked anxiously. "He was at our place?"

"He sent a package." Diamond's voice cracked a little. "I panicked. I was so stupid. I just turned. I didn't look." Diamond's hand tightened around Paul's, her eyes now bulging. "The other driver . . ."

"The other driver is fine, Diamond."

"I'm sorry." Diamond's voice was a whisper.

Paul stroked her forehead, and she closed her eyes again. After several minutes, Paul stood and began to pace.

Tara said, "If she received a package, it's got to be at the apartment. Unless it was in the car."

"I'll find out." Pause. "I swear . . . I told her. I warned her. She's a walking target."

Tara didn't know what to say. So she said, "At least she's going to be okay. That's all that really matters right now. We'll deal with the rest later."

Paul inhaled a deep breath, then released it. He nodded. "Yeah, you're right." He rubbed a hand on the back of his neck. "I just love her so much. I would do anything . . ." His voice trailed off. "Diamond has got to do some serious thinking when she gets out of the hospital. We can't ignore this threat any longer."

Tara couldn't deny that Paul was right. However, she wondered how Diamond was going to react.

Diamond loved her career, and she didn't want to give it up for anyone.

But would she give it up for her life?

Twenty-one

Shortly after ten-thirty that night, Tara entered her apartment. She kicked off her shoes, then dropped onto her sofa, a sigh oozing out of her as she did.

What a day.

But at least Diamond was okay, and as hoped, would be released from the hospital the next day.

Then what? Tara wondered. If her stalker knew where she lived, Diamond certainly wouldn't be safe.

He knew where Tara lived too, she remembered. At the very least, he knew her number.

There had been no strange calls recently, but she couldn't help feeling a spurt of panic as she wondered exactly what this creep was capable of. Would he be crazy enough to come to her place?

Tara suddenly felt very alone. She remembered the night Darren had come over, wanting to protect her.

She missed him.

Tara went to the bedroom. There, she saw the answering machine light flashing, indicating there were messages. She sat on the bed and hit the play button.

Two messages from Harris. He needed to see her, wanted to talk.

But the next message was from Darren. Tara perked up when she heard his voice.

"Tara, hi. It's ten o'clock. I'd hoped to reach you, but I guess you're busy." Pause. "I wonder." Deep breath. "I won't be back until tomorrow afternoon. You can call. If you want."

"Great, just great." Tara dragged a hand over her face. She'd just missed his call.

And judging by his message and the tone of his voice, he probably thought she was with Harris.

If only she had a number where she could reach him.

But he hadn't left one.

Tara did the best thing she could do. She called his home phone number. When his voice mail picked up, she said, "Darren, hi. It's Tara. I was at the hospital most of the day with my cousin. She was in a car accident, but she's okay. I'm so sorry I missed your call. I can only imagine what you're thinking, but you're wrong. I'll talk to you tomorrow."

Hopefully he would retrieve the message tonight.

Hopefully, her message would let him know that he had no reason to be concerned about Harris.

When Tara stepped into the office shortly after nine the next morning, she instantly saw the look of concern on Sharnette's face. Her stomach dropping, Tara followed Sharnette's line of sight over her shoulder.

Harris, who'd been sitting on a chair along the side wall, slowly stood.

Oh, Lord, no.

"I'm sorry," Sharnette whispered. "I lied, telling him you weren't coming in today, but he didn't believe me."

Tara was aware of David and Barry watching her as she crossed the room to greet Harris. How could he do this to her—come to her workplace and cause a spectacle?

"Morning, Tara."

"Harris." Tara shook her head as she looked at him.

"I didn't come here to argue with you," Harris said quickly.

"You shouldn't have come at all. I told you—I need time to think."

"I know." He paused. "Look, there's something I have to tell you. Is there somewhere we can talk?"

Tara glanced around. The only private office was Barry's, but Tara didn't want to ask him to use it. "You are putting me in a bad situation, coming here like this."

"Maybe we can step outside."

"Fine," Tara agreed. At least outside, no one would be able to eavesdrop.

The moment they were outside, Harris said, "I tried reaching you all evening, but you weren't home. Were you with your new boyfriend?"

"That's none of your business."

"It is—when he's the reason you're pushing me away."

"He is not the—" Tara stopped short. "I was at the hospital," she said, though she did not owe Harris any explanations. "My cousin was in a car accident."

"Oh. Is she okay?"

"She will be."

"That's good."

Tara folded her arms over her chest. "Harris, what did you want?"

"Have you heard from Darren?"

"Oh, please tell me this is not why you came here."

"Have you?"

"That is definitely none of your business."

"Maybe not mine—but what about yours?"

Tara blew out an exasperated breath. "I have no idea what you're trying to imply—"

"Did you know he went to Minneapolis?"

Tara's heart pounded at the name of the city where Darren had once lived. "Excuse me?"

"Minneapolis. Did he tell you he was going there?"

Tara steeled her jaw. "What's the matter with you? You had him checked out?"

"It's a simple question, Tara. Did he tell you or not?"

"I really don't feel like playing this game with you right now, but yes, he told me he was going out of town on business."

Harris laughed. "Business? That's what he said?"

Tara couldn't help feeling a spurt of anger. "You know, I've had enough of your games, Harris. I'm sorry that things didn't work out for you and Aisha, but that doesn't give you the right to try and mess up my life."

Ignoring her, Harris reached into his jacket pocket and withdrew a small white envelope. He extended it to Tara.

Tara took it from him, but didn't look at it. She

wanted to toss it on the ground, but something prevented her from doing so. "What is this?"

"Sometimes, the ones who seem the nicest are exactly the ones you should trust the least." Harris paused, then asked, "Don't you think it's time you knew the truth about your boyfriend?"

Darren had given Tara no reason to distrust him, and she felt like she was betraying him by even entertaining the possibility. Harris was the one who had hurt her. Anything he said she should take with a grain of salt.

"Look, Tara. I'm not the bad guy here. I'm a man . . . a man who loves you, but who made a bad mistake. We were together for five years. You know me. You know my best side; you know my worst side. This guy—what do you really know about him?"

Harris's tone softened. "Believe it or not, I was thinking of you when I did this. Of protecting you. I don't want to see you get hurt."

"Isn't that funny, coming from you?"

Harris's Adam's apple bobbed up and down as he swallowed. "I know it's hard to understand. I honestly never meant to hurt you. You can say I was temporarily insane, because I was. I just wish you'd forgive me, give us a chance to make a new start."

He sounded sincere, the way he had during the years they'd been together—the way he had the day he'd given her the promise ring at the airport. But he'd been lying then. He'd betrayed her.

Tara's gaze went to the envelope in her hand. "Darren has only been out of town a couple days. How could you possibly find out anything about him?"

"I've known about him for a little while."

"And that's why you suddenly wanted me back? Because you thought you were going to lose me?"

"Open the envelope."

Tara was suddenly afraid. There wasn't even the slightest hint of doubt in Harris's eyes, like he knew whatever information the envelope held would devastate her.

"I knew you wouldn't believe me if I told you the truth about him," Harris said, his voice full of chagrin. "That's why I got you this evidence."

Tara's hands shook. She couldn't open this envelope. Lord help her, she didn't want to know.

"Go away, Harris."

"You're going to need someone to help you get through this," Harris said.

Oh, God. What could it be?

"Whatever this is," she said, her teeth clenched, "it's a lie. It's something you've come up with to hurt me—because you couldn't stand that I was finally going to be happy."

"If you believe that, then why are you shaking?"

Anger engulfing her, Tara tossed the envelope at him then. "Leave me alone. You've already hurt me enough."

Tara whirled around on her heel and marched for the office door. But she stopped dead in her tracks when Harris said, "He's a murderer, Tara."

The strangest feeling swept over her, and she felt suddenly woozy, like she might faint.

Tara couldn't help it. She turned.

Harris blew out a weary breath before continuing. "There was no easy way to tell you this, Tara."

God, no. She hadn't heard him correctly. He was lying.

"But I told you because you deserve to know."

Harris stooped to pick up the envelope she'd tossed at him, then slowly started toward her. "Darren Burkeen, this guy you think is Mr. Wonderful—he killed his sister."

Twenty-two

For a moment, Tara couldn't move. She was completely rooted to the spot, transfixed with horror.

There was no way. Yet she found herself asking, "What did you say?"

"He killed his sister, Tara. The information is all in the envelope." Stopping in front of her, Harris gave her the envelope. "I knew I couldn't tell you something like that without proof."

Two beats passed before Tara tore at the paper. The first headline that jumped out at her read: *Teen Charged With Manslaughter in Sister's Death.*

The world started to spin wildly then, and Tara's knees buckled. Harris caught her before she collapsed.

"I'm sorry," he whispered, holding her tightly. "I know you won't believe that now, but I didn't want to see you hurt. That's the only reason I did this."

Tara looked down at the newspaper clipping. Then the next one, and the next. There was no denying that this was Darren. His picture was featured with two of the articles.

Tara's eyes scanned the last article. Key words popped out at her: *not guilty.*

But that didn't matter, not when he'd killed someone.

Tara couldn't help it. She broke down and cried, right there in Harris's arms.

He held her, rocked her, swayed with her, whispering softly, "I know, I know."

Harris had seen her home, given her a sedative, and tucked her into bed. There was no way Tara could stay at work that day, and while Barry and everyone else in the office had no clue what was going on—she hadn't dared tell them—they had concurred that in her state, she had better go home and get some rest.

Tara had slept fitfully for a least four hours, then abruptly woken from her slumber. The first moments of wakefulness, when her brain hadn't kickstarted the memory of what she'd learned, she'd been happy. Until she'd remembered Harris and how his visit had pulled the rug out from under her world.

Harris. Tara wondered if he was still here.

Climbing out of bed, she went to the living room. She saw him lying on her sofa. His eyes were closed, but the moment he heard her, they popped open.

"Hey," he said, sitting up. "You're awake."

Tara nodded grimly.

"How are you?"

"I've seen better days, definitely."

"I went shopping for you. You didn't have any food in your fridge."

"Oh. Thanks. You didn't have to do that."

Harris stood and walked toward her. "I know. But

I wanted to." He placed his hands on her shoulders. "I have a lot to prove to you."

Tara didn't respond. She felt numb. Harris may have truly regretted hurting her the way he had, but right now, that was the last thing on her mind. Tara could only think of the devastating news she'd learned, that Darren had killed his sister.

"Are you hungry? I can fix you something? Or I can order some Chinese from that place across the street you like so much."

Tara sighed. "Harris, I appreciate you bringing me home, for everything, really. But I need some time right now. I need to be alone."

Harris stared into her eyes for a long moment, then nodded. "Okay. I know you have a lot on your mind. Just know that I'm here for you."

"Thanks."

Harris kissed her cheek softly. Seconds later, he was gone.

After calling Diamond to make sure she was adequately settled at home, Tara took her phone off the hook. She didn't care who called; she wasn't interested in talking to anyone.

At work the next day, Tara was unusually silent. From the moment she'd walked through the door and given everyone curt greetings before heading to her desk, her colleagues had figured out that she didn't want to be bothered today.

And she certainly didn't want to engage in casual conversation, much less answer any questions.

Thank God no deliveryman came with flowers or chocolates for her. Tara was liable to shove any such gifts down the deliveryman's throat, just out of pure frustration.

She was through with romance.

Who needed it, when the person romancing you was a killer?

Oh, but she missed it. Missed what she'd become accustomed to. That's what hurt the most—that she had finally succumbed to Darren's charms, only for it to end the way it had.

He'd called, but Sharnette and everyone else had strict instructions not to put his calls through to Tara.

But by the afternoon, she realized that if nothing else, Darren owed her some answers. The man wasn't in jail, so there had to be a reason for that. While that thought gave her a measure of comfort, she still could not forgive him for keeping something so important from her.

"Sharnette, Darren may be calling for me. Put him through, okay?"

"Sure," Sharnette said, not asking any questions.

Back at her desk, Tara punched in his home number and left a message. About ten minutes later, Darren called.

"Hey, beautiful," he said. "I got your message a couple days ago, but I tried reaching you, and your phone was busy all last night."

"It was off the hook."

"Everything okay?"

Tara simply couldn't engage in any small talk. "I have to see you."

"Of course. I can come over later."

"No. Come here."

"To your office?"

"Yes." She didn't want to be alone with him in her apartment. "As soon as you can."

"All right. I have some time now."

When Tara looked out the window and saw Darren approaching the office, she jumped up from her chair and hurried to the door. She met Darren as he was opening it. Before he could say a word, Tara walked outside, leaving Darren no choice but to follow her.

Tara didn't stop walking until she'd rounded the side of the office complex's building. Here, there would be no traffic.

No distractions.

Hugging her torso, Tara exhaled a shaky breath.

"Tara, you've definitely got my attention."

Tara spun around. Her heart nearly split in two when she saw the concerned expression on his face.

"This is bad, isn't it? This is about your ex. You two are getting back together . . ."

"If only it were so simple."

A muscle in Darren's jaw flinched. "Whatever it is, just tell me. Don't sugarcoat it. Just give me the truth."

"Hmm. The truth."

"What?"

"I wonder why you didn't tell me the truth."

Darren eyed her warily. "What are you talking about?"

"I guess I know. How do you tell the woman you're sleeping with that you killed your sister?"

Surprise flashed in Darren's eyes. Disillusionment, even.

But not denial.

Good Lord, not denial.

A painful lump lodged in her chest. It was true.

Darren shook his head, staring at her with complete disbelief. "You had me investigated?"

"Wrong answer." Tara started off, but Darren took hold of her arm. Tara shrugged him off. "Don't you touch me."

"So that's just it—you bring this up; then you're going to run off?"

She looked up at him, into his dark brown eyes. Were these the eyes of a killer? "I'm not the one who lied to you."

"Is this what you do to every guy you date? Or only the ones who treat you decently?"

"You didn't think I had a right to know?"

"Right to know?" He gave her a hard look. "What exactly do you think you know?"

"I know that you killed your sister. I know that you were charged. And I know that you were found not guilty."

Darren could only shake his head, disappointment written all over her face. "Who told you this?"

"Why didn't you tell me you went to Minneapolis?"

"What—you've got a tail on me or something?"

Everything Tara had earlier ignored, like the strange call Darren had gotten at his place the morning after they'd made love, and the way he hadn't wanted to talk about his sister's death, hit her with full force. It all seemed so clear now.

"No, I'm not tailing you."

"Then someone told you this? Who?" Darren laughed, but the sound had no mirth. "Let me guess—your ex did this, didn't he? He wants you back, and he was willing to stoop this low. Yeah, that makes sense. Everything was fine, until he showed up at your door."

"It doesn't matter what he did. It matters that you lied to me."

"I didn't tell you."

"That's the same as a lie."

"Are you still in love with him?" Darren asked. "Is that what this is about? You want to make sure you think I'm the lowliest piece of dirt on the earth so that you can go back to him and completely forget about me, what we shared? No regrets?"

"A relationship needs trust."

"Exactly." Darren balled his hands into fists, then pounded them together. "Exactly." He blew out a harried breath. "You know what, you could have called me, you could have asked me what happened without practically accusing me of murder. You didn't. Your ex comes running back, only too happy to make me out to look like a villain, and you lap up his every word."

"I saw the articles."

"Did you?" Darren guffawed. "Then I'm even more surprised."

A beat. "What does that mean?"

"You seem to have it all figured out. Why ask me a thing?"

A weird feeling swept over her at Darren's words. She turned away as her breathing grew shallow. When she thought about it, she actually hadn't seen much of the articles besides the headlines and a couple of words. She'd been too devastated.

And Harris had filled in the blanks.

"Darren." Tara whirled around.

But Darren was gone.

Twenty-three

Darren's words haunted Tara for the rest of the day.

And the look in his eyes. The look of pure disappointment.

Yet if he was guilty of something so horrible, why should he have been disappointed in her?

Now, at home, Tara lay on her bed. Resting on her side, she squeezed one of the pillows against her stomach.

She was missing pieces of the puzzle, pieces only he could give her. But he wasn't answering his phone, and he wasn't calling her back.

Harris. Tara knew he hadn't made up the articles, but he no doubt had had time to read them, get the whole story. Why hadn't he left them with her so she could read them once she'd calmed down?

Because he'd only wanted her to see the scandalous headlines, and not the details of the story?

As much as she hated to admit it, Darren had a very good reason to be angry with her. She had approached him in an accusatory way, as if she were someone who knew the facts.

But what did she know?

She knew that if there was anyone she shouldn't

trust, it was Harris. Tara had loved Harris for five years, yet he hadn't honored her love. He had coldly dumped her without a second thought. When he'd learned that she was involved with someone else, he'd felt that proprietary masculine jealousy that Tara would never understand, and he'd realized then that he wanted her back.

Or maybe something else had happened. Maybe Aisha had dumped him. Or maybe he'd come to his senses and realized that he couldn't marry simply for position.

Whatever his reasons, Tara suddenly knew they didn't matter.

What she'd had with Harris was over.

If she hadn't met Darren, she might have taken Harris back—and then she would have been back in a relationship that wasn't as fulfilling as she now knew relationships could be. With Darren, Tara felt incredibly alive. Just one of his looks made her entire body tingle with longing.

She was in love with him.

Tara rolled onto her back, closing her eyes. A long breath seeped out of her.

Wow. It was true.

Perhaps she'd known from the first time Darren had left town. She'd missed him every single moment that he was gone. And when she'd seen him again, she'd felt complete in a way she never had with Harris.

But with the memory of her earlier relationship haunting her, Tara had tried to keep her feelings at bay, hoping to protect her heart. Now, she could no longer deny the truth.

She knew she was in love with him, because right now, she realized that no matter what had happened with his sister, she believed in her soul that Darren hadn't maliciously set out to hurt her. She *knew* it. Every time she'd looked into Darren's eyes, she'd seen nothing but sincerity. And a hint of pain.

She'd exploited that pain. Whatever had happened had devastated him, and she'd thrown that in his face.

Man, this hurt. She felt like the cruelest person in the world, rejecting the one man who had shown her nothing but a blissful world of romance and love.

It was a world she now knew she wanted without a doubt.

But was it too late? Had she blown her chances at happiness forever?

"Hey, Tara."

"Diamond." Tara walked into her cousin's arms, her eyes misting with tears.

Diamond embraced her. "Hey." Surprise sounded in her voice. "What is it?"

"I blew it," Tara said, feeling utterly helpless. "I blew it."

"Come in," Diamond told her, breaking the hug.

Tara wiped at her eyes. "Is Paul here?"

"No. He's working evenings this week."

"What's going on, sweetie?"

"God, Diamond. I feel like a fool. Harris wanted me back, and he dug up this dirt on Darren . . . and I believed him. I practically accused Darren of being a murderer." Tara raked a hand through her hair. "Gosh, you don't need this right now. You're going through your own drama."

"Whoa. Are you sure I wasn't in a coma for a

week? What the hell has gone down in such a short amount of time?"

When Tara answered her question with a whimper, Diamond took her by the hand. "Come on in."

Diamond led Tara into the living room, where they both sat on the sofa. "All right. Tell me everything."

Tara did, starting with Harris's arrival at her apartment, his bombshell that Darren was a murderer, and Darren's utter disappointment in her over it all. "I didn't even talk to him. I just started in on him, going on an on about what I thought I knew."

"Well," Diamond began cautiously, "obviously, something happened. It makes sense that you'd be curious."

"Curious, yes. But I didn't even read the articles. I saw the shocking headlines, and I formed my own conclusions. That's exactly what Harris wanted. I'm such a moron."

"Don't be so hard on yourself. Harris manipulated the situation. He manipulated you."

"I know. . . ."

"So, what are you going to do?"

"I've called Darren. But he's not returning my calls. I can't say I blame him."

"You really care about him, don't you?"

"I'm in love with him."

"Whoa. And I thought I was the one who bumped my head."

Tara giggled. "Shut up."

A smile touched Diamond's lips. "I'm not surprised. From everything you've said about him, I knew it was only a matter of time."

"But what if I've blown it?" Groaning, Tara settled back on the sofa, resting her head on the headrest.

"I don't think so," Diamond said. "Not if Darren is as wonderful as you say he is."

"I don't know . . ."

Diamond asked, "Have you eaten anything today?"

"No."

"Well, you're going to need your energy to think of a way to get through to Darren. That requires food."

Tara lifted her head. "Food?"

"Mmm-hmm. How can you think on an empty stomach?"

"I'm not really hungry."

"How about a pizza?"

"You're not listening to me."

Diamond smiled sweetly. "That's right. So, pizza?"

Tara knew there was no point arguing. "Sure."

Diamond jumped up from the sofa. "And you know what? I'm gonna grab you a pair of pajamas. You're staying here tonight."

"No, that's not necessary. I don't want to impose."

"Impose on what? You haven't been here in ages. And Paul's not even here to object. Besides, I think he wouldn't mind. At least I won't be here alone while he's working."

"Oh, gosh. I'm so sorry. Forgive me, Diamond. I haven't even asked what's gone on since you came home from the hospital."

"Nothing much. I'm taking it easy. There hasn't been anything else crazy going on. Paul had an alarm system installed."

"That's why it took you so long to open the door."

"Mmm-hmm. So, we're safe." She paused. "The police have the package. They're getting prints from it, or whatever they do in a situation like this."

"But nothing yet."

"No, nothing yet."

Diamond smiled. "But you know what, tonight, you and I are going to forget about our problems. We are going to have a good old-fashioned sleep-over, complete with pizza and sodas, and ice cream—just like we used to do when we were young."

Tara's lips lifted in the slightest of grins. She couldn't deny that Diamond's suggestion made her feel a hundred times better. And she definitely didn't want to spend the night alone in her apartment.

"That sounds wonderful," Tara admitted.

"Remember when we were young, and didn't have a care in the world? Except you were always pining over that guy Jeremy."

"Huh! I was not."

"Sure. Deny it now. I know the truth." Diamond made a silly face.

Tara laughed, and so did Diamond.

"See, we're already having a good time."

"Yes. You're right."

"Tonight, we'll be silly. Tomorrow, once you're adequately rejuvenated," Diamond continued, "you can decide what to do next."

Tara breathed in a slow and steady breath. "Tomorrow is Saturday. Darren shouldn't be work—"

"Shh." Diamond stood in front of Tara and

placed a finger against her lips. "Not tonight, re-member?"

Tara slowly stood, then wrapped her arms around Diamond. "I love you, you know that."

"I love you, too."

The night's sleep did Tara a world of good. She awoke with a renewed sense of hope.

If Darren truly loved her, they could get past this. Sooner or later he would come around. He would realize, as she did now, that he needed to give her a chance to explain—the way she should have given him a chance to explain.

And if he didn't . . . well, then they didn't have the kind of love to get them through the trials and tribulations of life.

She still had questions for him, too, which he had to know. But this time, she'd ask, not accuse.

"I want to thank you for putting up with me," Tara said when she stood at the door with Diamond.

"You know I'm here for you," Diamond assured her. "The same way you've been there for me when I needed you."

Tara nodded. "I know."

"Are you sure you don't want to join me and Paul for some breakfast? His treat . . ."

Diamond's eyes twinkled, and Tara was happy to see her cousin in good spirits. "No. You two enjoy your breakfast. Cherish this time you have to-gether."

"All right." Stepping toward her, Diamond wrapped her arms around her dearest cousin. "Lis-ten, drive carefully. And call me to let me know when you get home."

"I will." Tara planted a kiss on her cheek, then pulled away.

Tara reached into her purse for her key. Closing her hand around it, she gave Diamond a smile and was about to turn. Instead her eyes met Diamond's once again.

"Diamond?"

"Yes?"

"I want to say something. I know we're already family—we're cousins. But I couldn't love you more if you were my flesh-and-blood sister."

"I know, sweetie. I feel the same way."

Tara did know. Diamond had told her on numerous occasions that she felt closer to her than she did to her own sister, Marcia. And being an only child, Tara had always considered Diamond her sister.

"And I guess I realized . . . even if things don't work out with me and Darren, I've still got it good. I have the best family I could ask for. And the best cousin a girl could ever want. That makes up for a lot."

Emotion overwhelmed Diamond, and a tear escaped her. "Oh, great. Look what you made me do." Diamond wiped at the tears.

Tara hugged her. "It's true." And it was. Having family you could rely on was the most important thing in the world. "I think I can handle anything . . . as long as you're in my life."

"That's such a sweet thing to say." Diamond pulled back, brushing away more tears. "You know I feel the same way. And you know I'm always going to be in your life, so don't even think otherwise."

"You better be." Now Tara was crying, too. "No more crazy car crashes, okay?"

"Okay."

"Now go enjoy breakfast with your man."

"I will. And call Darren, Tara. I know you two can work this out."

Twenty-four

"Darren, hi. I don't know if you've gotten my messages. Well, I'm sure you have. I hope you've had time to think, and that you now believe how sorry I am for how I brought this whole thing up. I really am. But there's something else I need to tell you, and I was hoping to tell you in person. I guess I'll just have to tell you like this." Pause. "I don't know what happened with your sister, but, Darren, I know you didn't do anything to hurt her. At least not deliberately. I know that you couldn't. And I know it must be terribly hard for you to deal with whatever it is. Please call me. Please, let's talk."

Darren's chest tightened as he listened to Tara's message, his resolve crumbling. This message was different from the earlier ones she'd left. This time, she'd said the one thing that mattered most.

She didn't believe he'd deliberately hurt his sister.

Darren didn't realize how important it was for him to hear those words from her until he felt warmth spread through his body.

And his heart.

He closed his eyes, slowly reopened them. Tara *was* special. He had known it from the moment he'd first seen her.

This proved it.

She could so easily have stayed angry with him—or at the very least, disillusioned. Given what she'd learned, he understood that she had questions. Another woman would have held on to her pride, insisting that she had done nothing wrong.

Not Tara.

"What are you waiting for?" he asked himself.

Darren snatched the receiver from beside his bed and dialed Tara's number.

Tara placed the receiver at her ear and said, "Hello?"

"Tara, hi. Listen, I can't talk right now, but if you don't hear back from me in ten minutes, call me back."

"Diamond, where are you?"

"I'm at home." She spoke in a hushed whisper. "And I don't want Paul to hear me. If you call back and I answer, then everything's fine. If you call back and no one answers, or if Paul doesn't call me to the phone, then you know something's wrong."

"Diamond, what on earth is going on?"

"I'll explain later."

Then Diamond hung up.

Tara stood, dumbfounded.

When the phone rang a moment later, Tara instantly snatched up the receiver. "Hello."

"Tara. Hi."

Darren. Tara's heart melted. "Hi."

"I got your message. Messages."

"Um. You did?"

"Yes."

"That's good. That's great." Tara was preoccupied because of Diamond's call. "I'm sorry. I want to talk to you—I really do. But it's just that I got a weird call from my cousin—"

"Everything okay?"

"That's just it. I don't know."

"What did she say?"

"It's more what she didn't say that has me concerned," Tara explained. A sick feeling was spreading over her. "I think my cousin is in trouble. She said to call her in ten minutes . . . but I have to go. Now."

"To her place?"

"Yes. Something's wrong. I feel it."

"I want to go with you."

Tara thought for a split second before saying, "Can you meet me at the plaza at Kendall and one-forty-seventh in five minutes?"

"Sure."

"I'll see you then. You can follow me to her place."

Diamond couldn't quite put her finger on what had made her come to this conclusion, but as she watched Paul sitting in the living room, watching TV the way he normally did on the weekends, the premonition grew stronger and stronger.

She needed to know the truth, and there was only one way to find out. But how would she bring it up?

How would she ask him what she feared in her heart?

Diamond slid into the armchair. Paul hardly seemed to notice her, that's how involved he was with the sports program on the television. Diamond didn't mind, because she was still racking her brain for the clue she was missing.

Her stomach lurched. It suddenly hit her.

It was the picture.

The picture that had been vandalized in the box.

Yes, that was it! How had she not realized sooner?

Somehow, she managed to keep her composure, though her stomach was a painful ball of knots.

She remembered the event. She had been hosting a charity function at a school in Coconut Grove. Paul had been there with her that day. He had taken pictures of her from the crowd.

Her breath caught in her throat. Could she be right? Was that what was nagging at her subconscious?

Yes, she was sure of it. Ninety-nine percent sure.

She remembered the photo because it was one that Paul had told her he loved; he'd loved the expression on her face as she'd been oblivious of the camera. But after he'd taken the pictures two months earlier, Diamond hadn't seen them again. He'd meant to put them in an album.

And Diamond had put the photos out of her mind.

Until now.

"Paul." She wasn't sure how she was going to bring it up, but suddenly the words "You're the one who's doing this to me, aren't you?" slipped from her lips.

Paul's eyes shot to hers. "What'd you say?"

"You're the one who's doing this to me."

"What are you talking about?"

Diamond slowly stood. "It makes sense. God help me, I don't know why you did it—"

"Did what?"

"The letters. The calls. The roses in my car. That *picture.*"

Instantly, Paul was on his feet. "Do you hear yourself? You sound crazy, Diamond. Of course I didn't do this. How could you even suggest something so crazy? I'm a cop."

When Paul stepped toward her, Diamond backed away. "The police said it had to be someone close to me, that that was the only thing that made sense. You know where I work, you of course know where I live. And you know Tara. How would any stalker know about her? I don't mention her or any of my family members on the show, because I want to protect them—"

"If—if someone was following you, they—they could easily have seen you and Tara—together—then followed her as well." But he was fumbling over his words, so unlike him. "That's what makes sense, Diamond."

"Maybe . . . but that's a little far-fetched."

"Not for someone who's determined."

Diamond stared into Paul's eyes. They were stony, unreadable.

"Just tell me. I will feel so much better knowing that no one is out to get me or my family."

Paul didn't say a word, but something flashed in his eyes. Something that scared Diamond.

"Oh, God." She'd confronted Paul with this theory, hoping to prove it untrue. But the detective was right. It *was* someone close to her.

It was Paul.

Diamond whirled around on her heel, hurrying to the apartment door. But Paul was fast on her heels, gripping her upper arm with firm fingers.

Diamond's determined eyes met Paul's. "Let me go, Paul."

"No, Diamond. I don't want you to leave. Not like this."

"You can't expect me to stay. Not now."

"You don't understand," was all Paul said in reply.

Diamond gave her arm a tug, but still Paul didn't release her.

The phone rang. Diamond threw a glance in its direction.

Tara . . .

"Damn!" Tara exclaimed, tossing her cell phone onto the seat beside her. Her cousin wasn't answering. And that could only mean one thing.

Something bad.

What was going on?

Tara glanced in the rearview mirror as she drove north along the turnpike. Darren was still behind her. He had been at the shopping complex before she'd gotten there, and seeing him, Tara had motioned for him to follow her, then quickly gotten back on the road.

She wanted to talk to him, but the drive to Diamond's was not the right time. She and Darren needed a time where there would be no distractions, and they needed a quiet place.

Tara reached for her cell phone and once again called Diamond. Once again, the phone rang until the answering machine picked up.

Tara disconnected the call and hit the gas. She was almost at her cousin's place in Coral Gables.

* * *

"You need to calm down, Diamond."

Paul's words, though spoken in a cool voice, sent a chill of fear racing down her spine.

If Paul was crazy enough to be the one stalking her, then Diamond had no clue what he was capable of. She had to play it cool.

"All right," Diamond said in the most steady voice she could manage. "I'm calm. Will you please let go of my arm?"

Paul eyed her cautiously. "You're not going to run?"

"No."

Paul slowly released her arm, as if trying to gauge her next move. But when she didn't make a move to leave, Paul completely let her go. Diamond brought a hand to her arm where he'd squeezed, gently massaging it.

Beside her, Paul started to pace. Diamond simply watched him, assessing his demeanor. Waiting.

"I love you, Diamond." He stopped. Faced her. "I love you. And all I've ever wanted to do is protect you."

Diamond didn't know what to say that wouldn't make the situation worse, so she said, "I . . . I believe you."

"The thought of someone hurting you . . . That's why I hated you doing the show. You didn't care about all the negative attention you got, but I saw where it was leading. To another Clay situation. And I didn't want to see you hurt." He walked a few steps forward, pivoted, then retraced his steps. "I certainly never wanted to hurt you." His eyes met hers. They were filled with desperation. "You believe that, don't you?"

He reached for her, and Diamond did everything

in her power not to flinch. Gently, he ran a finger along the bruise on her forehead.

"It was killing me, how you were slipping away. Because I love you so much."

Diamond heard pain in his voice. Guilt. And she heard all the words he wanted to say but couldn't.

In that moment, she didn't know if Paul was crazy, or if he was simply a guy who loved her who'd made an incredibly stupid mistake.

"I did get hurt," she said softly, looking away.

"I know. God, I'm so sorry about the accident."

"I could have been killed."

"I never expected it to go this far." He released an angst-filled breath. "I just . . . I just wanted to show you . . . I wanted you to need me. The way you did in the beginning."

When Diamond looked up at him again, tears glistened in his eyes.

He said, "You were slipping away . . ."

"Oh, Paul."

It was the calls to Tara where Paul had messed up. After receiving the package, Diamond had done some serious thinking. Remembering the calls Tara had received, and remembering the detective's words that the culprit was probably someone close to her, Diamond had wondered if Paul could truly do this. In the pit of her stomach, she'd had the uneasy feeling that she was right. Something had bothered her about the package, but at the time she didn't know it was the picture.

Diamond knew what she'd say to a woman if she called her show and told her this story—she'd tell her to call the police and have her boyfriend arrested as soon as possible. But in reality, making tough decisions like that were never easy.

Especially since as she stared at Paul, at the look of shame in his eyes, she knew he truly hadn't meant to hurt her. He'd somehow gotten caught up in a twisted plan.

And it had almost worked. Diamond had seen such a caring man in Paul once again when he'd been by her bedside in the hospital.

But it was all based on a lie.

Now, she simply felt sorry for him.

"Diamond." His voice was filled with pain as he walked toward her. "Can you forgive me?"

He opened his arms to her, and after a few seconds, Diamond walked into his embrace.

"Huh, Diamond? Can you? I know, I totally messed up . . ."

"Paul." Her voice was full of regret. "I'm sorry too. Maybe I held back in our relationship and that frustrated you." She knew that was one of her flaws; after her relationship with Tyrone, she had done everything in her power to protect her heart. "But I could have been killed. Even if I can forgive you, I can't . . . I can't forget that."

Paul held her tighter, and though she couldn't hear him, Diamond felt his body tense and release as he cried. So she held him, saying good-bye to him with that hug, in that moment.

A minute later, there was pounding on the door. Paul pulled apart from Diamond, surprise flashing on his face.

"That's . . . that's probably Tara."

"Will you get rid of her? I just . . ."

Diamond merely shrugged, then went to the door. Paul didn't try to stop her.

Diamond was surprised to find not only Tara outside her door, but a man with her.

"God, Diamond. You're okay? I was so worried!"

"I'm all right," Diamond said softly. Her eyes went to the mystery man. "Is this who I think it is?"

"Oh, that's right. You haven't met him. Yes, this is Darren." Tara glanced over her shoulder at him, then back at Diamond. "Tell me, what is going on?"

"Come in." Diamond stepped back and held open the door. To her surprise, when she looked around, Paul was still there.

Paul looked at Tara and Darren, then back at Diamond. "You're leaving, aren't you?"

Diamond nodded. "But not yet. Tara, Darren—will you guys wait out here? I want to talk to Paul in the bedroom."

"Sure," Tara replied, but she looked at her with concern.

"I'll be fine."

Then she took Paul's hand and led him into the bedroom.

Twenty-five

"Well." Tara blew out a quick breath. "What a day this has been." After Diamond had left her and Darren in the living room, she'd spent the next half-hour or so in the bedroom with Paul. Tara had been shocked to see Diamond come out with a packed suitcase.

And she was even more surprised by the story Diamond told her once they had left the apartment.

The only bright spot was knowing that there wasn't a deranged stalker out there who truly wanted to harm Diamond. Tara was still concerned about what Paul might do, but Diamond was one hundred percent certain that Paul would do nothing further to hurt her.

"He wanted to get my attention," Diamond had said. "He wanted to be my hero. But it all went too far."

"You sure you don't want to call the police?" Tara had asked.

"He's a cop himself. If this comes out, it will ruin his career. But he knows he has to stay away from me, because if he doesn't, then yes, I will report him."

After that, Darren and Tara had seen Diamond

to her parents' place; then they'd headed back to Tara's apartment. With her cousin's crisis out of the way, Tara had only her situation to think of—and how it would turn out.

Now, she sat on one side of the sofa and Darren sat on the other.

"Yeah, what a crazy story," Darren commented. "But at least it's all been resolved for the better."

"I still can't believe Paul. How could he do that? The guy's a cop."

"I don't know. People are crazy, sometimes."

Tara didn't respond, and silence settled over the room. She looked at Darren, but he was looking at the floor.

Finally, Tara spoke. "Will you tell me . . . about your sister?"

Darren's eyes closed for a long moment. When he opened them, he didn't speak right away. Tara was wondering if he ever would when he said, "It was an accident. A horrible, horrible accident. And that was hard enough to deal with—until I was charged."

"What happened, Darren?"

"My sister and I and one of her friends had been at a party. People were drinking—my sister and Emily included. I hadn't been, but I'd gone to the party after working all night at a factory and being up all day.

"I was exhausted, and I never should have gone to the party, and when Emily demanded that we leave because she had to be home by midnight, I should have made her get a taxi. Instead, we all got in the car and while I was driving Emily home, I fell asleep at the wheel." Pause. "The next thing I know, the car was hitting a tree.

"The passenger's side sustained the most damage. My sister—she—she was ejected—"

Instinctively, Tara slid across the sofa and took Darren's hand in hers.

"I didn't tell you because it's so hard to talk about. I see my sister's body . . . she wasn't wearing a seat belt."

"Oh, Darren." Easing closer to him, Tara wrapped his head and held it to her chest. "How horrible. I'm so sorry."

Several moments passed, the only sounds in the room Darren's labored breathing.

"I feel like such a fool," Tara said.

"Emily was the daughter of one of the city councilors. Her father insisted on charges. He tried to say I'd been drinking, but I hadn't been."

"What happened to Emily?"

"She was paralyzed from the waist down. Her family was outraged, but it was an accident. Emily's father started this huge smear campaign in the local papers, hoping that public opinion would find me guilty. In the end, it didn't work. The jury knew it was an accident. . . ."

"People always look for someone to blame." Tara shook her head ruefully. "They didn't even consider what you were going through. How much guilt you had to be feeling."

"I was the only one who walked away." Darren looked at Tara then. "Why me?"

She stroked Darren's head. "There's no point asking that kind of question. Only God knows the answer to that."

Darren's shoulders drooped as he exhaled. "She's still paralyzed, but she's been undergoing experimental treatment at a hospital in Minneapolis.

That's why I've gone there recently. I wanted to show my support. . . . In a way, being there for Emily . . . it's almost like being there for Tracy."

Tara held him close to her again. "Darren, forgive me. Please. I am so sorry that I contributed to your pain. . . ."

As she kissed his temple, Darren put an arm around her waist. Tara stilled. Darren pulled his head back and looked into her eyes.

"Are you still in love with Harris?"

"No," Tara said without reservation. "I'm not in love with him anymore . . . because I'm in love with someone else. And I guess in a really strange way, Harris's stunt finally made me realize that."

Darren turned on the sofa, positioning himself directly in front of Tara. "You're in love with someone else?"

"Yes. Darren, I'm in love with you."

A grin broke out on his face. The next second, he had her face in his hands. "Tara, do you mean it? Really?"

"God, yes. No one has ever made me feel the way you make me feel. You make me feel secure. You make me feel so loved . . ."

"I love you," Darren whispered.

And then his lips were on hers, softly at first, but the kiss soon erupted into one that spoke of passion and need.

Tara broke the kiss. The heat that burned in Darren's gaze made her body quiver with longing.

"Everything was moving so fast," Tara said. "I know now that I was afraid."

"I'm sorry I scared you."

Tara put a finger on Darren's lips. "No. No, don't

be." Her mouth curled in a soft smile. "Sometimes, there are things you just know."

Darren bit down on his lip, then asked, "And what do you know?"

"I know that you're the man who was born for me. And I was born for you. And I don't want to waste any time being apart, when I know in my heart that we will be together forever."

Relief passed over Darren's face. "Oh, baby. I knew it. I knew it in an instant."

"And now I know it."

"Kiss me," Darren whispered.

As Tara leaned close and pressed her mouth against his, she knew without a doubt that this was right.

That they had the kind of love that would last for a lifetime.

Epilogue

Six months later . . .

Tara strolled into her town house, a smile on her lips. She always walked into her new home with a smile, ever since her marriage to Darren last month on Christmas Day.

She had every reason to smile, and no reason to frown.

The day she'd learned that Harris had hurt her beyond her wildest imagination, she never would have expected to be so happy with someone else less than a year later.

But here she was, living out her own dream come true.

Harris, having learned he'd lost Tara forever, had ended up marrying Aisha Harmon after all.

Tara didn't care. Not one bit. She cared only about Darren, the man of her dreams.

"Sweetheart?" Tara called.

There was no answer.

Tara kicked off her shoes and started into the house. She'd assumed Darren's car was in the garage, but maybe he had gotten called out for work.

That was fine by her. It would give her enough time to prepare a special dinner for her man.

Tara strolled into the kitchen, and was about to open the fridge when she noticed the wall phone's message light was flashing. She picked up the receiver and dialed the code to retrieve the messages.

"Tara, hi. It's Diamond." Pause. "I can't believe this. I swear, I just can't believe this."

Tara's heart leaped to her throat.

"I found out today that Clay has escaped from the mental facility. And given the items in his room, the police are pretty certain that he's going to try to contact me.

"They're worried, Tara. And so am I." Loud sigh. "I can't go through this again. I just can't. And I wanted to let you know . . . I won't be anywhere you can find me. I have to get away. I have to stay safe. Until they catch him."

Then the message ended.

Tara stood, rooted to the spot on the kitchen floor, fear spreading through her entire body.

Clay.

Oh, Lord. He'd escaped.

Diamond was in trouble.

And she was on the run.

Dear Readers:

IN AN INSTANT is the first of two stories that features the Montgomery cousins—Tara and Diamond. As you know from having read this book, the two are as close as sisters, even though they are quite different. Tara is down-to-earth and has a five-year plan for where her life will be, and Diamond is spontaneous, opinionated, and fun—which is why she's doing so well as a radio talk show host.

IN AN INSTANT features Tara's love story, in which this practical woman is swept off her feet when she least expects it. I truly hope you enjoyed Tara and Darren's story as much as I enjoyed writing it.

I couldn't help giving you a glimpse into my next BET book—Diamond's story. As you can guess, her story, tentatively titled IN A HEARTBEAT, will be full of romance and suspense. Watch for it sometime in early 2003.

Until next time, happy reading!

Kayla